Shadows of the Silver Screen

Christopher Edge

Albert Whitman & Company
Chicago, Illinois

Library of Congress Cataloging-in-Publication data is on file with the publisher.
Text copyright © 2013 by Christopher Edge
First published in the UK in 2013 by Nosy Crow Ltd.
Published in 2014 by Albert Whitman & Company
ISBN 978-0-8075-7319-8

Printed in China.
10 9 8 7 6 5 4 3 2 1 BP 18 17 16 15 14

For more information about Albert Whitman & Company,
visit our web site at www.albertwhitman.com.

For my mum

I

The corridor was shrouded with shadows, its dark walls flickering with an almost-spectral impermanence. The only light cast on the scene came from a glowing candelabra gripped in the hand of a woman in white. With a shudder, she stepped toward the corridor's end, the silent swish of her long gown gliding noiselessly across the floor. There, a door stood slightly ajar; the open crack an invitation for the darkness to creep in.

A low murmur of music seeped through the frame, an organ thrum that filled the ominous silence. Black hair cascaded over the woman's shoulders, framing her deathly white features. With her free hand, she reached for the door handle, her fingers trembling as if in fear of what she would find within.

As the organ music swelled in warning, a dark shadow fell across the woman's back. She turned in horror, her mouth gaping wide in a silent scream.

This was echoed immediately by a shrill chorus of shrieks as the face of a man loomed large. His gnarled hands reached out with murderous intent and the candelabra fell to the floor, its last flash of light silhouetting the two figures locked in a deadly embrace before darkness fell across the scene. The music rose to a swirling crescendo and the words *FIN* filled the screen.

Leaping up onto the raised stage in front of the screen, a frock-coated showman brandished a bullhorn, his bushy whiskers almost as untamed as the riotous red of his coattails.

"That's all, ladies and gents," he called out, his voice booming through the tent. "Make your way to the exits, please!"

As the curtains across the exits were pulled back, letting the evening sunlight stream into the tent, the audience rose from their seats, the air of entrancement that had been cast by the cavalcade of moving pictures slowly fading into memory. An excited babble of voices battled to be heard as their owners shuffled toward the light, every set of eyes as wide as saucers at the marvels they had seen.

"Here, I leapt out of my seat when I saw that feller spring up. What a horror!"

"I know, I thought he was going to strangle me himself!"

"A most remarkable performance—one could've almost believed it was real."

Near the rear of the tent, a young girl in a stylish tailor-made suit slowly rose to her feet. Her long dark hair brushed past the collar of her jacket, its light-green serge perfectly matched to the color of her eyes. Next to the girl, the lanky figure of a boy was already standing, his own jacket of a decidedly more threadbare design.

"So what did you think, Penny?" The boy scratched his scruffy mop of blond hair in wonder, a broad grin of excitement spread across his face. "Wasn't that the most terrifying thing you ever have seen?"

Raising an eyebrow in surprise at her friend's enthusiasm, Penelope shook her head.

"I'd hardly call such a hackneyed collection of scenes terrifying, Alfie," she replied scornfully. "Haunted castles, witches' cauldrons, mad monks, and swooning women—the makers of this moving picture show have just stolen ingredients from every gothic tale ever told and thrown them together onto the screen with no regard for the plot. If I printed a story like this in the pages of the *Penny Dreadful*, Montgomery Flinch's name would be mud."

As the orphan heiress of the *Penny Dreadful*, Penelope Tredwell had transformed the fortunes of this once fourth-rate literary magazine, turning it into a bestselling sensation. Published in its pages behind the pseudonym Montgomery Flinch, her tales of terror had entranced more than a million readers and made Montgomery Flinch into one of the most celebrated authors of the age. Only a few people knew the real identity of the renowned Master of the Macabre, and as the printer's assistant on the magazine and Penelope's very best friend, Alfie was one of them.

"All right, so maybe the story wasn't up to much," Alfie conceded as the two of them trailed the tail end of the crowd toward the exit. "But what does that matter when you feel as though you are really there? The picture's the thing! I heard that at a show over at Hampton Court Fair, half the crowd fainted when they saw a ghost train rushing towards them out of the screen. These filmmakers can make you believe that anything is real."

A crush of picture-goers still milled around the exit to the tent, seemingly reluctant to leave in case the wonders they had seen on screen sprang into life again. Their gleeful voices mingled with the cries of the fairground hawkers outside.

"Ladies and gentlemen, step this way please for the fright of your life. Don't be afraid to experience the phantasmagoria of fear!"

Digging his elbows into the jostling crowd, Alfie barged a path for them through the throng. Penelope quickly followed behind him, rapping the knuckles of a scruffily dressed boy as his fingers snaked opportunistically toward her purse. Then the two of them emerged from the shadow of the tent, blinking in the sunshine that still warmed the sky even as evening slowly slipped toward night.

Before them the summer fair was in full swing, a state of perpetual bustle and noise spilling across the fields of High Barnet. Crowds of people surged between the attractions, all in search of the ultimate thrill. Nearby, a volley of shrieks erupted from the swirling gallopers of the merry-go-round, the riders whooping as their carved steeds rose and fell at dizzying speeds. With a clang, steam swing boats swung back and forth, a gaggle of young urchins lurking nearby in case loose change fell from the pockets of those on board. And beyond the Razzle Dazzle, helter-skelter, and switchback rides, yet more novelties filled the fairground, all eager to separate the crowds from their money: circus booths, boxing shows, fortune-tellers, and menageries of exotic beasts. The warm air hung heavy with the heady scent of spiced nuts and pickled whelks.

As Alfie tugged on Penelope's arm to pull her into the heart of the fray, she glanced back at the fairground cinematograph show, its grand facade screening the interior of the tent from view. Carved angels twined around ornate golden columns, while a backdrop of luridly painted scenes hinted at what waited within. In the center of this elaborate frontage a towering organ pumped out a queasy tune of welcome as a new stream of visitors hurried up the steps, their eyes wide in anticipation. The sign above the entrance read:

Penelope frowned. Was this all that people wanted from their stories nowadays—a second-hand fright in the dark?

Turning, Alfie saw Penelope still staring back at the ornate facade. "We can line up again if you want to see the show a second time," he told her. "I wouldn't half mind watching it again."

"I really don't want to sit through that nonsense again," Penelope replied. "I'm just surprised that so many do."

"But all the fairs have got moving pictures now, they're ever so popular. I even heard that they're thinking of opening a cinematograph show on Shaftesbury Avenue itself."

Penelope shuddered at the thought of such a shameless novelty springing up among the glittering theatres of London's West End. Her thoughts crept back to the pages of the *Penny Dreadful*. She had to show that stories still mattered, much more than mere spectacle. The next issue of the magazine would have to cast this passing fancy into the shade. She would show her readers what fear really meant.

Penelope looked up at Alfie, her pretty green eyes sparkling with resolve. "We need to catch the next train home."

Alfie's face fell. "But we've only been here a couple of hours," he grumbled. "The fair stays open until late."

Penelope shook her head firmly. "I need to start work on the August edition of the *Penny Dreadful* right away. This new story I'm planning from the pen of Montgomery Flinch needs to be something big; an epic tale of terror that will have the nation scurrying beneath their bedclothes in fright."

Alfie sighed. He'd hoped that by bringing Penelope along to the fair, they could both escape the long shadow of the *Penny Dreadful* for just one evening. But now a reminder of the printer's proofs piled up on his desk awaiting his return crept into his brain.

"Just one more ride on the velocipedes?" he ventured hopefully, knowing the answer even before he asked.

"We really need to be getting back," Penelope replied. "Else Mr. Wigram will start to worry."

At the mention of Penelope's guardian, Alfie immediately nodded his agreement. He didn't want to get on the wrong side of the stern-faced lawyer, who was also his employer on the *Penny Dreadful*.

"You're right," he said. "Let's go."

They set off through the fair, heading across the tramped-down field for the railway station that lay just beyond the far line of trees. Screams and shouts of excitement followed their every step as they weaved their way through the crowds. The noise of a dozen fairground organs competed for attention as they squeezed past a row of brightly painted booths, ignoring the hawkers' cajoles and ducking behind a wheezing generator.

Gradually leaving the hubbub behind, Penelope and Alfie followed a ragged line of fairgoers traipsing down the path that led toward the station. Immediately in front of them, a swaying couple leaned against each other for support, their senses dulled by the day's entertainment.

Alfie glanced toward Penelope. "So what's this new story of yours going to be about, then?" he asked with a smile. "Are any mad monks or haunted castles going to make an appearance?"

Penelope grinned. "I think I'll leave that kind of story to the cinematograph show," she replied. "The power of the printed word can find more subtle ways to shock." Behind her smile, the beginnings of a story were already starting to take shape in her mind.

II

"It's quite intolerable. I can't go on like this!"

His face flushed, the man drew himself to his feet, towering over Penelope's desk in the cramped office of the *Penny Dreadful*.

Penelope looked up from the papers scattered in front of her, fixing a weary smile to her face. She glanced across at her guardian, Mr. Wigram, who was seated at his desk at the rear of the office, sunshine slanting in through a high window and falling across his face. With his silvery hair blanched almost white by the light, Mr. Wigram blinked hard and then frowned, his own annoyance written across his features.

"I can't go anywhere—speak to anyone—without that blasted Montgomery Flinch getting in the way. They follow me, you know!" the man exclaimed, reaching into his jacket pocket for a handkerchief. "Some have even stooped to sneaking up on me in the sanctuary of my own club, thrusting their grubby scraps of paper into my hand for me to sign. It's got to stop."

As he paused to wipe the sweat from his brow, Penelope saw a chance to put an end to his rant.

"Monty, you knew perfectly well what you were getting into when you signed the agreement. As the public face of Montgomery Flinch, it's only to be expected that some of our avid readers will wish to share their enjoyment of his stories with you. You need to attend to their inquiries with the courtesy and grace your position demands."

"But the questions they ask," Monty moaned. He slumped back down into his chair as quickly as he had risen from it only moments before. "'Mr. Flinch, what was the secret of the Withered Man?' 'Mr. Flinch, how many times did the Dread Mare rise?' 'Mr. Flinch, where exactly did *The Tale of the Shattered Heart* take place?'"

Monty gripped the arms of his chair in a flash of anger. "How am I supposed to know!" he hissed, his knuckles whitening as he stared back at Penelope. "I didn't write the damn things!"

At that moment, Alfie emerged from the back office, carrying an armful of galley proofs. Sensing the air of tension that filled the room, he glanced from Penelope to Monty. The actor's usually jovial face was clouded with fury, his eyes flashing darkly beneath bristling eyebrows. Alfie tiptoed to his chair, slid the proofs onto his desk, and then settled back to watch the show.

Penelope frowned, a slow worm of worry burrowing into her brain. This wasn't one of Monty's usual weekly moans that could be soothed with a few words of praise or the promise of a raise to his contract. This was a full-blown actor's tantrum and would need careful handling. She couldn't risk even a hint of Montgomery Flinch's true identity reaching the ears of anybody who wasn't in this room.

"Mr. Maples—" Wigram started to speak, but Penelope raised her palm to show she had the situation in hand.

"I'm sorry, Monty, but the contract you signed with the *Penny Dreadful* was an exclusive one that allows us to retain the sole rights to your superb theatrical services," she began, her tone of voice a soothing mix of flattery and threat. "The generous weekly fee that we pay you is to reflect the fact that playing the part of Montgomery Flinch is a full-time role."

"Full-time would be fine," Monty replied with a groan, "but this part is taking over every second of my life. The author tours, public readings, book signings, and after-dinner talks. If I'm not careful, I'll forget who I really am. Monty Maples, the finest actor of his generation snuffed out at the hands of Montgomery Flinch." He held his head in his hands, his mournful eyes fixing Penelope with a beseeching stare. "I need a break."

Penelope sighed. Monty was no use to her like

this. In his present mood, the actor was a walking stick of dynamite waiting to explode. All it needed was for someone to ask for his signature at an inopportune time. A rash response from Monty could bring Montgomery Flinch's carefully crafted reputation crashing down in ruins.

Maybe it would be best to allow him a short vacation—a trip to a spa town perhaps—to restore his good spirits. The *Penny Dreadful* could afford to pick up the bill. She reached for her desk diary. They would have to cancel Montgomery Flinch's scheduled engagements first, concoct some story about the author retreating to the country to work in solitude on his latest tale. A faint smile crept across Penelope's lips. With Monty out of the way for a while, it might even give her some time to write it.

"If you wanted a holiday, Monty," she said, "then you only needed to ask."

The actor's eyes widened in surprise at Penelope's unexpected reply; then he sprang forward from his chair to seize her by the hand.

"Thank you, my dear, sweet girl!" Monty declared, a broad grin clearing the clouds from his brow. "I knew you would understand. I'll only be away for a mere month and then I'll return to play the part of Montgomery Flinch with aplomb."

Wincing, Penelope tried to retrieve her fingers from Monty's grasp.

"Wait a second, what do you mean a month?"

she replied in a flustered tone. "I was proposing a week's vacation—a trip to Bath, perhaps, to sample the restorative waters there. The costs of this will be paid by the *Penny Dreadful* but of course deducted from your future fees."

Now it was Monty's turn to wince.

"But I need longer than a week," he said. "The tour of the provinces is scheduled to last for the whole of August."

As soon as the sentence had slipped from his lips, Monty clasped his hand to his mouth, suddenly realizing that he had said too much.

"What tour of the provinces?" Penelope demanded.

A look of guilt momentarily flashed across Monty's face. Then he threw back his shoulders as if casting off a weight, his appearance taking on a determined air as he met Penelope's gaze.

"That's what I've been trying to tell you. I need a break from the role of Montgomery Flinch," he announced. "I'm an actor. I want to sing, to dance, to astound an audience with the full range of my theatrical skills, but instead I find myself reading these same macabre tales night after night. It's enough to drive a man to drink."

Monty clasped his hand to his chest as though the strain was almost too much to bear. Reaching into his jacket pocket, he drew out a plain postcard, bearing the familiar stamp of the telegraph office.

"When I received this telegram from an old

actor friend of mine, I knew it was the answer to my prayers. He has invited me to appear in his production of *The Pirates of Penzance*, playing the leading role of the pirate king. It's just the tonic I need—far more soothing for the soul than any week away in a spa town. Once the tour is completed, I will return refreshed and ready to light up literary London again."

The corners of his mouth creased into what Monty hoped was a winning smile. "Besides, surely a month's leave can be arranged. It is the summer after all."

Penelope sat dumbfounded at her desk. Her slender fingers whitened as they gripped the pencil in her hand. Monty was actually serious about this.

"Are you mad?" she asked, her voice incredulous. "Montgomery Flinch is known throughout London as the Master of the Macabre. We've created one of the most celebrated authors alive today: a man of mystery, danger, and intrigue. How would it look if he appeared on stage dressed like Blackbeard himself, singing 'Oh, what a glorious thing, to be a pirate king'? You would ruin everything!"

As Alfie tried to stifle a laugh, Monty bristled with indignation.

"I hardly think that Seymour would have cast me in the show if he thought I would be its ruin."

"Not the show," Penelope fumed. "I'm talking

about the *Penny Dreadful*. We've got more than a million readers eagerly waiting for the next serial to fall from the pen of Montgomery Flinch. If just one of those readers was to discover that he wasn't who he claimed to be, the scandal would make the front page of every newspaper in the land."

"But it's a tour of the provinces," he protested. "Nobody there will have even set eyes on Montgomery Flinch. I'll use my own name—a pseudonym even—I just have to get back on the stage!"

"It's out of the question," Penelope replied firmly. "There's no way we can let you take such a risk."

His dark eyes flashing angrily, Monty threw his arms wide in exasperation. "Then I quit!"

As the words left his lips, Penelope stared up at him in shock.

An eerie calm fell over the office. Mr. Wigram shook his head with an inaudible sigh as Penelope and Monty glared at each other, both silently seething at this position they now found themselves in. Then the silence was broken by a knock on the door.

For a second, nobody moved. The door knocker rapped again, twice in quick succession, and Alfie jumped up from his desk and hurried to it. He opened the front door to reveal a man in a pinstripe suit standing on the doorstep, jauntily tapping his walking stick in time to the tune he was humming. Behind the man, a mouselike woman peered from beneath her parasol, its white-laced fringe shading her plain features from the sun.

"Can I help you, sir?" Alfie asked.

The man leaned forward, peering around the doorframe to inspect the office within. He was a tall and well-built man, just setting out on the journey into middle age. His handsome suntanned features were framed by red-tinged whiskers, which gave his face a vulpine cast. Spotting Monty standing in the middle of the office, he turned back toward Alfie with a broad smile.

"I'm here to see Montgomery Flinch," he replied, his voice as smooth as his countenance. "I've come to make him an offer he can't refuse."

III

Brushing past Alfie, the man strode into the office as though it was his own. His eyes darted around its interior, mentally photographing every element on display—the dusty bookshelves, the desks filled with scattered page proofs, typewriters, and all the familiar accoutrements of the magazine trade—before he bounded up to Monty and grasped him by the hand.

"Mr. Flinch, what an honor to meet you at last," he exclaimed, pumping Monty's hand in a hearty handshake. "Please allow me to introduce myself. I am Edward Gold, the proprietor and president of the Alchemical Moving Picture Company. I've come here today to present to you a proposition that will transform your literary fame into cinematographic stardom."

From the doorway, the man's companion had shuffled apologetically into the office, lowering her parasol to reveal a homely face framed by locks of dark-brown hair. The man glanced back and, snapping his fingers, gestured for the young woman to join them.

"This is Miss Mottram, my secretary," he continued, as the woman half curtsied in front of Monty. "She has in her possession the contracts I've taken the liberty of drawing up to show the seriousness with which I make this offer to you, Mr. Flinch."

Miss Mottram fumbled at the catch to her leather valise, then drew out from the bag a hefty sheaf of papers. She thrust these into Monty's hands with a simpering smile.

Puzzled, Monty glanced down at the papers, his gaze almost immediately glazing over.

"Ahem!"

With a pointed cough, Mr. Wigram rose from his chair at the rear of the office. "If I may interrupt," he said with a frosty tone, "I am Mr. Flinch's legal representative, and as such, all inquiries of this nature should be directed to me. Mr. Flinch is a very busy man and certainly has no time to speak to you today. If you care to leave your proposition with me, I will consider it in due course, but for now, sir, I must bid you good day."

With a tap of his cane, the filmmaker turned toward Wigram and fixed the lawyer with the full beam of his wolfish smile.

"I would be delighted to set out my proposition to you all," he announced. "I want the world to hear how I will put Montgomery Flinch's name up in lights at the front of every cinematograph show. I am going to make him a moving picture star."

Wigram's brow furrowed, lending his features a pinched and disapproving air. "Mr. Flinch is a serious writer," he replied stonily. "Not some fairground performer. I would suggest that you take your proposal elsewhere. It is of no interest to us—"

Raising his hand, Monty waved the elderly lawyer into silence. A strange gleam seemed to shine in the actor's eyes.

Behind her desk, Penelope looked on, powerless, almost holding her breath in fear of what Monty might say next. He'd told her that he'd quit. She prayed that he wouldn't give Montgomery Flinch's secret away.

"Let's not be too hasty, William," Monty began, an intrigued smile spreading across his face. "You've got to admire the pluck of the fellow in coming here today. And besides, I could do with a diversion from my latest grim tale." He turned back toward the filmmaker. "How exactly do you propose to make me a star of the silver screen, Mr. Gold?"

With a flourish, Gold unbuttoned his jacket; the sunlight slanting in through the high window putting him into the spotlight.

"The Alchemical Moving Picture Company is one of the leading practitioners of the art of the cinematograph. Our moving picture shows have entranced audiences from Abbey Wood to the Uxbridge Fair."

As the filmmaker spoke, Miss Mottram stared up at him, her eyes wide in adoration.

"But the times are changing," Gold continued. "The crowds are starting to tire of the same old cinematographic shows—the films of tortoise races, donkey derbies, and boxing bouts. The flickering scenes of everyday life no longer suffice. They are eager for more crafted forms of entertainment. Some have tried with feeble spectacles of terror, limp frights that go bump in the night. But the audience thirsts for more substantial fare. Stories of mystery, drama, and suspense; a tale of truth that will hold them spellbound as they huddle in the dark." The filmmaker fixed Monty with an unflinching stare. "Stories like yours, Mr. Flinch."

Penelope glanced across at Alfie. Her friend's mouth gaped wide with excitement, already imagining the pages of the *Penny Dreadful* brought to life on the cinematograph screen. But an uncomfortable shiver ran down Penelope's spine. She hadn't worked so hard to write the stories of Montgomery Flinch just to see them turned into cheap entertainments. It was time to take control of this situation, before things got out of hand.

"What exactly are you proposing?" she asked in a clipped tone.

Gold glanced down at Penelope, as if noticing

her for the first time. His eyes flicked over her face as if framing her for a close-up shot and, for a second, his expression froze. Then, with a forced smile, he replied.

"Why, to bring one of Montgomery Flinch's finest fictions to the silver screen, of course. I propose to make a film of *The Daughter of Darkness*."

Penelope was struck dumb by his reply. *The Daughter of Darkness* was one of the very first stories she had written under the pen name of Montgomery Flinch.

Set amid the wild moors of Devon, this tragic tale of murder, betrayal, and revenge told the story of Alice Fotheringay, the only daughter of the widowed Earl of Taversham. With her mother dead, Alice is kept almost prisoner by her father in the gilded cage of Taversham Hall, waited on by a retinue of servants. The earl's fortune comes from the vast copper mines that lie under the sprawling lands of his ancestral estate. These mines are worked by local villagers; men, women, and children alike, whom the earl rules over with a rare cruelty. One day, when Alice escapes from the manor house, she finds herself lost on the moors but is rescued by Oliver, a young boy who works down one of her father's mines. To guide her home, Oliver gives Alice a present of a strangely carved stone he has unearthed from the depths of the mine, but when the earl discovers this, he flies into a rage and storms off to confront the boy. When Oliver is discovered dead in the mine the very next day, Alice knows her father is to blame. Pouring out her hatred, she stares into the heart of the stone and the darkness within creeps into her soul, filling her with a terrible power…the power to bring Oliver back. When the dead return, they wreak a terrible revenge on those who have wronged them—as the Earl of Taversham discovers to his cost…

When the tale was first published in the pages of the *Penny Dreadful*, the reviews had been somewhat sniffy. While all showed admiration for the power of Montgomery Flinch's prose, many reviewers had found the subject matter somewhat sensationalist. However the enthralled readers of the *Penny Dreadful* didn't agree with their verdicts and the magazine's sales had shot through the roof.

As Penelope now tried to order her thoughts about Mr. Gold's unexpected proposition, Monty was ready with his answer, his face flushed with excitement.

"A wonderful idea!" he declared. "And would there be a part in this moving picture for me to display my own thespian talents? You may have noticed that my performances of dramatic readings from my stories have found favor with the public. I recently sold out five nights at the Royal Albert Hall!"

"You must have been reading my mind, Mr. Flinch," Gold replied, half bowing in deference to the author's quick thinking. "I wanted to offer you star billing: the part of the earl himself, no less. With the power of your performance, you will have the audience hanging on your every word, their eyes fixed to the screen as you portray the cruelty of this villain's dastardly deeds."

"Wait a minute," exclaimed Alfie, suddenly sitting up in his chair, "the cinematograph shows are silent. How will they hear what Monty—I mean Mr. Flinch—says?"

Turning to face the printer's assistant, Mr. Gold rapped his cane on the office floor before pointing it at Alfie like a wand.

"The young gentleman is right," he replied. "But trust me, Mr. Flinch—I do not intend to make you stand in front of a camera holding up a board that spells out your script!"

At this quip, his secretary laughed coquettishly, the shrill sound halfway between a squeak of a mouse and the hiss of an owl.

Frowning momentarily, the filmmaker dropped his cane back to the floor before continuing his explanation. "At the Alchemical Moving Picture Company, we have invented a new form of cinematograph. A camera that can record and project both picture and sound—the Véritéscope! This trailblazing innovation will transform our moving picture shows and the stories we are able to tell."

He turned back to face Monty, a messianic gleam

in his eyes. "With this wondrous invention, I will take the cinematograph show out of the traveling fair and instead set up screens on every high street. Crowds will eagerly queue outside town halls, assembly rooms, and variety theatres to see the marvels of sight and sound combined."

Gold glanced across at Wigram, who was still staring at him with suspicion.

"Of course," the filmmaker continued, "if you agree to this proposed adaptation, it will be to both our benefits. At your public readings, Mr. Flinch, I have heard that you perform to as many as five thousand people in a single night. However, with the hundreds of prints I plan to make of this film, you can play to tens of thousands every night without ever leaving the comfort of your club as *The Daughter of Darkness* is exhibited across the country. And what's more, the magnetic power of your performance will be captured for posterity to delight future generations, even after we are all dead and gone."

With this final appeal to Monty's vanity and Wigram's wallet, Gold brought his impassioned speech to a close.

For a moment, the office fell silent; then Monty turned toward Penelope with a wide-eyed expression of delight etched across his features.

"What do you think, Penelope?" he boomed. "Want to see your old uncle's stories shimmer across the silver screen? A capital plan, don't you think?"

As every face in the room turned toward her, Penelope shifted uncomfortably in her chair. She stared back at Monty, spotting the mischievous twinkle in his eyes that told her he had her trapped. There was no way she could say no without risking revealing the truth about Montgomery Flinch. Her gaze darted to the broad-shouldered figure of Mr. Gold, the filmmaker leaning nonchalantly on his cane, his easy smile betraying the fact he thought this was a done deal.

Penelope's mind raced as she tried to think through a solution to this intractable situation. If this new-fangled Véritéscope was everything that Mr. Gold claimed, then perhaps a film of *The Daughter of Darkness* could be of some benefit. It might help bring her tale to a whole new audience but, more importantly, it could keep Monty onside.

As she looked up at Monty's smug smile, a slow smile of her own crept across her lips. The wily actor might think he had her over a barrel, but Penelope had him just where she wanted. This cinematographic diversion was the perfect way to cast to one side all thoughts of him prancing across the stage in *The Pirates of Penzance*. Instead, Monty could satisfy his thespian desires on the screen in the role of the villainous earl.

Smiling sweetly, Penelope finally nodded her

head. "It certainly sounds like it," she replied. Penelope turned her head toward the filmmaker, her eyelashes quivering as she fixed him with an awestruck gaze. "We really must see this wondrous invention for ourselves."

IV

"Are you sure that this is a good idea?"

Wigram removed his top hat to wipe his brow with a handkerchief. The mid-morning sun was already roasting the pavement, and the elderly lawyer shifted uncomfortably beneath the mantle of his frock coat. A fresh bead of sweat was descending down the creases of his frown as he addressed Penelope again. "This cinematographic fancy is a most unwelcome distraction from our preparations for the August edition of the *Penny Dreadful*. We are already behind in our deadlines for commissioning this month's illustrations."

Penelope glanced up at her guardian, the delicate bloom of her features shaded from the sun beneath a broad parasol. "I promise to attend to the illustrations immediately on our return to the office," she reassured him, "but this visit to the Alchemical Moving Picture Company is of importance too. A successful cinematographic adaptation of *The Daughter of Darkness* could bring yet more readers to the *Penny Dreadful*, whilst, as we've already discussed, this venture is proving to be a useful way of keeping Monty happy with his lot."

Her guardian glanced down at his fob watch again. "Speaking of Mr. Maples," he sniffed, "he's late."

Penelope glanced up the narrow street. The walkway was lined with shop fronts, the signs hanging outside every doorway speaking of the trade that had made this street their home: *Hepworth and Co. Camera Company, Optical Magic Lantern and Photographic Suppliers, Gaumont Film Studios, British Mutoscope and Biograph Company, the Kinematographic Club.*

This street was Cecil Court or, as the hansom cabdrivers now called it, Flicker Alley. Above the shop fronts, the grand Georgian buildings reached up for four more storeys, and behind each set of windows sat yet another cramped office belonging to one of this new breed of filmmakers, plotting to turn their cameras on the world. But outside on the pavement, Penelope could only see a couple of scruffy delivery boys, sweating as they pushed their heavy barrows down the street. There was still no sign of Monty.

Lowering her parasol, Penelope swept her long dark hair back from her face. Her pretty green eyes sparkled with certainty.

"He'll be here," she replied confidently. "Monty's very keen to see his name up in lights on the cinematograph screen."

"Humph." Wigram peered at Penelope with a pointed expression. "If I didn't know you better, Penelope, I'd almost suspect that this was your motivation too."

Before Penelope had a chance to respond, a shout from the direction of the Charing Cross Road turned both their heads.

"Penelope! Mr. Wigram!"

Stepping down from a hansom cab, Monty was already hurrying toward them. His cheeks were flushed as his heavy frame bustled down the road, the tails of his morning coat swinging behind him.

As Monty reached their side, he panted out an apology. "Terribly sorry for my late arrival," he wheezed. "I'm afraid I was caught up at my club. My friend Seymour was in town last night and I simply had to make amends for the mix-up over my part in his production of *The Pirates of Penzance*."

Penelope pursed her lips. "I do hope you didn't reveal the reason for your refusal. If anyone was to learn that—"

Monty waved her concerns away. "This was Seymour's first trip to London in years. He doesn't take a newspaper or even a magazine, so he's hardly going to connect me to Montgomery

Flinch. Besides, he's heading back to Hull tonight."
Puffing out his cheeks, the actor clapped his hands
together. "Anyway, I'm here now."

Sighing in exasperation, Penelope turned away.
She looked up at the number above the door
tucked to the side of the nearest shop front: 22
Cecil Court. According to Mr. Gold's business
card, this was the place where the *Penny Dreadful*
would take its first steps into the world of film.
Next to the door, a peeling nameplate listed the
tenants whose offices lay within. Stepping toward
this with Monty and Wigram in close attendance,
Penelope's eyes flicked down the list; one name
stood out, its letters scribed in the freshest coat of
gold paint.

THE ALCHEMICAL MOVING PICTURE COMPANY.

"Shall I do the honors?" Monty inquired, his
hand poised above the door knocker.

Penelope shook her head. "Remember what I
said. Let Mr. Wigram do the talking. We don't want
you agreeing to sell the rights to *The Daughter of
Darkness* for a few magic beans."

With a disgruntled harrumph, Monty stepped
back to let the lawyer rap smartly on the door.
After what seemed like an interminable wait, the
door opened a crack and a sour-faced woman
peered outside.

"Yes?"

"Good day, madam," Wigram began, clutching
his top hat in his hands. "I am seeking the premises

of the Alchemical Moving Picture Company. We have an appointment with its proprietor, Mr. Edward Gold."

Leaning out the door, the woman scrutinized the nameplate that Penelope herself had been inspecting only moments before.

"Oh, him," she sniffed, spotting the freshly painted name at the bottom of the plate. She pulled the door open and then stepped back inside, folding her bare arms across her stout chest. "Up those stairs, second door on the right. That's where you'll find him."

Nodding his head in gratitude, Wigram led them inside. The landlady eyed Penelope suspiciously as she stepped over the threshold, her beady gaze following the three of them as they headed for the stairs. Unlike the street outside, the dingy hallway was filled with gloom. Boxes of camera equipment and mechanical contraptions were piled higgledy-piggledy everywhere they looked. Cameras, projectors, arc lights, and winders, the cramped hall seemingly an Aladdin's cave of the picture show.

Clambering past the boxes, Penelope fell into step beside her guardian as they climbed the creaking staircase. She heard a sharp exclamation behind them and glancing back, saw Monty wincing in pain, his toe stubbed on a crate of film stock. Shaking her head, Penelope trailed her hand along the banister as they climbed but then lifted it in dismay to inspect the layer of dust that now clung to her fingers.

"I do hope that this new invention of Mr. Gold's is in better repair than his premises," she said, extracting a handkerchief from her pocket to wipe her hand.

Wigram raised a skeptical eyebrow. "That remains to be seen."

At the top of the stairs, a dismal corridor burrowed into the heart of the building and, as a still-grumbling Monty joined them, they walked its length. Passing by the offices of the *Kinora Camera Company* and the *Bioscope Press*, Penelope came to the second door on the right. A nameplate reading *The Alchemical Moving Picture Company* was fixed next to the door handle but etched into the pane of frosted glass in the door were the words *Graham & Latham Cinemascope Suppliers*, the G of the first word somewhat faded as if someone had tried to scrub the letter away. Behind the glass, two shadowy silhouettes were visible, and, from within, Penelope heard the sound of a raised voice with what seemed like a foreign accent.

"I've come for what is rightfully mine!"

Wigram raised his hand to knock on the door, but she quickly motioned for her guardian to wait.

Another voice was raised in reply, and Penelope recognized the smooth tones of Mr. Gold now transformed into a snarl.

"You signed the contract—that camera is

mine. Now get out of my office before I have the constabulary remove you!"

There came the sound of a muffled curse followed by heavy footsteps, and Penelope quickly stepped back from the door before it was flung open. A man wearing a shabby gray blazer stood framed in the doorway. He was in his early thirties, his dark-brown hair cut short in the Continental style, while his pointed beard gave his face a sharp expression. He glared at them over his half-moon spectacles.

"I'm terribly sorry, sir," Penelope began. "We've come to see Mr. Gold."

The man's eyes filled with venom. "*Zut pour vous!*" he spat, brushing past Penelope with a snarl and stomping off down the corridor.

"What a nerve," Monty began, shaking his fist at the departing figure. "I've a good mind to—"

Ignoring Monty's bluster, Penelope knocked lightly on the now open door. Inside the office, Miss Mottram cowered behind a desk piled high with papers, and at Penelope's knock, the secretary turned in fear toward the door. Spotting Monty and Wigram standing by Penelope's side, she quickly rose to her feet and hurried toward them.

"Mr. Flinch," she squeaked, holding the office door open. "What an honor to see you here, sir. Please, do all come in."

Monty bowed his head in greeting as he entered the office, with Penelope and her guardian following closely behind. With a nervous glance into the corridor, Miss Mottram shut the door firmly behind them.

Casting her eyes around the room, Penelope took this opportunity to inspect the offices of the Alchemical Moving Picture Company. At first glance, her impression was not a favorable one. Apart from a couple of peeling posters advertising five shilling box cameras, the walls of the cramped room were bare with not even a window to let in the daylight. The room was lit by a foul-smelling gaslight that hung from the low ceiling. In front of the secretary's desk was a plain wooden chair, and the only hint of luxury came from the leather-upholstered armchair in the opposite corner of the room, from which Mr. Gold now rose.

The easy charm of his smile curling his lips, Gold stepped toward Monty and clasped his hand in his own. No sign now of the anger Penelope had heard in his voice through the glass.

"Mr. Flinch!" exclaimed the filmmaker. "How good of you to grace us with your esteemed presence." Releasing Monty's hand, he gestured apologetically at their poky surrounds. "I'm only sorry that our current premises aren't as steeped in literary history as your fine offices at the *Penny Dreadful*. However, in time I'm sure this address will hold a similar luster as the place where the film career of Montgomery Flinch was launched."

Monty beamed in delight, fresh thoughts of film stardom beginning to bloom inside his mind. However, the sound of a cough behind him quickly punctured these dreams.

"That is yet to be agreed, Mr. Gold," said Wigram as he appeared at Monty's side. "Mr. Flinch would first need to see proof of these grandiose claims you have made for your new invention." The lawyer glanced around the office, a look of haughty suspicion in his gaze. "Does this 'Véritéscope' even exist yet?"

Smoothing his whiskers, Gold nodded his head.

"Of course, I quite understand," he replied. "Indeed, I am as eager to show you the wonders of the Véritéscope as you are to see them and have taken the liberty of filming a short scene from the story. Once you have observed the remarkable power of this medium, I am sure you'll appreciate what a sensation a moving picture of *The Daughter of Darkness* will create."

The filmmaker paused, noticing Penelope for the first time as she hovered in the background, her downward gaze slyly inspecting the papers on his secretary's desk. "I must admit though I hadn't realized that this screening would attract so young an audience today." His flint-gray eyes glittered in the glow of the gaslight. "I would have arranged for suitable refreshments if I had known."

Following the filmmaker's gaze, Monty glanced back to see Penelope as she stood there smiling sweetly, the cerise of her stylishly cut jacket and shirtwaist putting the office's drab decor to shame.

"Ah, yes," Monty replied, in an almost too-eager tone. "I've brought my niece, Miss Penelope Tredwell, along here today. She is a keen admirer of the cinematographs and so I would value her opinion on the merits of your Véritéscope show. I trust this is acceptable to you?"

"Quite acceptable," Gold replied, turning the full beam of his smile toward Penelope. He took her hand in his own. "I'll be delighted to hear your thoughts, Miss Tredwell."

The filmmaker's fingers felt slippery to the touch and Penelope blushed under the intensity of his gaze. Lowering her eyes, she nodded primly. "I look forward to seeing my uncle's story on the screen."

As Wigram looked on with a well-worn frown, Gold released Penelope's fingers from his grasp and then turned toward the rear of the office. There, a door stood slightly ajar, revealing another room beyond this outer office. Ahead of her employer, Miss Mottram hurried toward this, a circular metal canister clutched in her hands.

"Now, if you'd all care to accompany me to the screening room," the filmmaker announced, "I'll present you with a first glimpse of *The Daughter of Darkness*—a moving picture that will transfix the world!"

V

In the crepuscular gloom, Penelope shifted uncomfortably in her chair, its hard wood and keen edges sending an unpleasant tingle up her spine. Beside her, Wigram sat in silence, his brow furrowed as he stared impatiently at the whitewashed wall that lay before them, while from the chair directly to her right Penelope heard a strange rustling sound. Turning her head, she watched as Monty unwrapped a boiled sweet, noisily discarding the wrapper before popping the striped lozenge into his mouth. Feeling her eyes on him, Monty glanced across, his gaze meeting Penelope's glare. Then he reached apologetically into his pocket and, extracting another hard candy, held it out toward Penelope.

"Humbug?" he asked.

Penelope shook her head with a sigh.

Behind them, at the rear of the room, Gold fussed over a strange-looking contraption that stood upon a tripod, its long lens pointing toward the whitewashed wall. The lens was protruding from a large box made of mahogany and brass, a small door on its side held open as Gold fixed the reel of film in place, nestling it between a morass of spokes and sprockets, tubes and strange frills. Finally satisfied, he closed the door with a click, the Vérитéscope now ready to screen this promised glimpse of *The Daughter of Darkness*.

"As I explained, Mr. Flinch," Gold began, the sudden loudness of his voice from the shadows making Penelope jump in her seat, "I've so far only filmed a brief opening scene, but I trust it will give you a sense of the power of this remarkable invention."

The filmmaker gave a nod toward Miss Mottram. Standing by the dimmed gas lamp that was fixed to the wall, his secretary pulled at its chain to cut off the flame, plunging the screening room into darkness. As Penelope glanced back over her shoulder in surprise, there came a whirring, clicking noise from where Gold had been standing and then a beam of silver light sprang forth from the lens of the Vérитéscope, bathing the wall in a sepia hue.

Turning again to the makeshift screen, Penelope watched as this sepia hue slowly softened into a golden glow. Swirling shapes drifted like mist across the wall, oddly different to the harsh black-and-white lines she had seen at the fairground picture show. Fascinated, Penelope watched as these shapes finally coalesced into recognizable forms, a frozen scene suddenly lifelike on the screen.

She gasped. The picture that filled the wall showed the same room they were sitting in. Blank whitewashed walls, their chairs now standing empty as the guttering gas lamp cast a flickering light on the scene. It was as though the screen had become a mirror instead, casting their shadows out as it imagined the world anew. But what really took Penelope's breath away were the vivid colors she could see, the picture trembling with an uncanny reality.

Even though the room on the screen was empty, Penelope couldn't pull her gaze away. Sitting in the darkness, it somehow felt more real to her than this same room she was sitting in. She watched as the figure of a woman stepped onto the screen.

A summer shawl was draped over the young woman's shoulders, shrouding the elegant blue silk of her evening gown. She turned to face the camera, dark locks of hair framing a sad-eyed stare. A shiver of recognition ran down Penelope's spine. This was Miss Mottram, the mousy secretary who scurried behind Gold everywhere, somehow miraculously transformed by the camera lens.

Her gaze pierced the screen, some secret sorrow troubling her countenance. Then she began to speak.

"I am the daughter of darkness," she began, the sound of her words somehow appearing in the air as they trembled from her lips. "And this is my story—a tragic tale of murder, betrayal, and revenge."

Penelope's mouth fell open, shocked to hear the words from her story spoken on-screen.

Beside her, she felt Monty lean forward in his chair, a low mutter of astonishment escaping from his lips. "Incredible…"

But Monty's murmur was swept into silence as from the screen the young woman spoke again. "Ever since Mama died, I've lived here with my father on these lonely Devon moors. This grand house is my home, my playground, my prison. My father says he must protect me from the evil that lies beyond these walls, but I know now that the cruelty that lies beneath the moors is his alone."

A single tear ran down her cheek, its glistening trail shimmering in the silvery light. Staring up into the face of her own creation, Penelope was enthralled.

"This half-life of mine would be hard enough to bear without the misery I have seen. At my father's mines, children toil in the darkness, chained and harnessed like dogs as they drag from the depths the copper that has made his fortune. Dressed in ragged clothes, they crawl through tunnels buried deep in the earth, never glimpsing the sun from morning to night. From my father's carriage, I have watched them rise from the pit, wreathed in shadows of steam. I shudder to think of their suffering, those poor, godforsaken souls."

As they spilled from the screen, her words seemed to thicken the air around them. The whir of the Vérytéscope was replaced by a distant hiss, the foul stench of steam rising to their nostrils. On the chair next to Penelope, Wigram sniffed into his handkerchief, while on her other side, Monty's shoulders shuddered with tears; the hardships the girl described were almost too painful to hear.

"My father professes not to care," she continued. "He says that the money he earns from the mines pays for the finery of my clothes and the banquets that we eat. But my heart chafes at his cruelty and the food on my plate tastes like ashes in my mouth."

On the screen, Miss Mottram's dark eyes glittered as she opened her hands to reveal a jet-black stone.

"Deep in the mines, the darkness lies," her voice revealed in a trembling tone, "and it has given me a gift of this stone."

Sitting in her chair, Penelope felt a strange sensation creep up her spine, the shadows cast across the screen almost hypnotizing her as she stared up into the darkness.

Then, from the back of the screening room came a sudden snapping sound, like a spring or a coil breaking. The image on the screen froze and then disappeared in a blaze of white light that faded as quickly as it had come. For a second, there was silence and then, with a gentle whoosh, the gas lamp fixed to the wall spluttered into life, shedding its light on the scene.

Slowly shaking her head as if waking from a dream, Penelope glanced around the room. Next to her, her guardian was still staring at the whitewashed wall, his brow furrowed as if trying to work out what trickery they had just seen, while, with an ashen face, Monty turned toward Penelope with wonder in his eyes.

"It seemed so real," he murmured.

At the rear of the room, Gold stood over the box and tripod. The small door on the side of the camera hung open as the filmmaker fiddled with the tubes and sprockets inside. Then, finally shaking his head in defeat, he looked up to meet Penelope's gaze.

"I'm afraid a slight technical problem has brought today's screening to a premature close," he announced, "but I hope what you have already seen has shown you what a film I will make."

Stepping toward them as Monty rose from his seat, Gold unleashed the full brilliance of his smile. "I assure you, Mr. Flinch, that the wonder of the Véritéscope will craft the raw materials of your story into a cinematographic sensation. So, what do you say? Do we have a deal?"

Monty beamed with glee but then glanced apprehensively at Penelope as if fearing her reply.

Penelope's mind was still filled with the shadows that had flickered across the screen, so unlike any cinematograph show she had ever seen. She turned toward Wigram, a frown still troubling her guardian's face as he met her gaze.

"We have to make this film," she whispered.

VI

"I must strongly advise you against signing this contract, Penelope."

Wigram peered over the foolscap pages as he laid out the agreement on Penelope's desk. The sheaf of papers was at least an inch thick, the corners of practically every page turned down with notes scrawled in the margins.

"This isn't an agreement, it's a travesty," he declared. "You'd be lucky to see even a penny of any profits Mr. Gold makes from this cinematographic fancy."

He turned the pages of the contract, pointing out his litany of concerns as Penelope stared blankly at the dense and impenetrable text.

"There isn't a clause in this contract that isn't stuffed with sharp practice and underhand maneuvers." The frown lining Wigram's face deepened, its creases becoming crevasses. "In all conscience, Penelope, speaking as both your lawyer and your guardian, I must insist that we withdraw from this arrangement with Mr. Gold and cease all plans for the Alchemical Moving Picture Company to film this adaptation of *The Daughter of Darkness*."

Penelope glanced up at her guardian and saw the look of concern in his eyes. Ever since her parents died, Mr. Wigram had been by her side. His had been the comforting hand that had helped steer her through her grief, his wise counsel preventing the *Penny Dreadful* from falling into the hands of her late father's creditors. And as she had built the magazine into the towering success it was today, Mr. Wigram had been there every step of the way, protecting her interests and safeguarding her secret. Penelope trusted his counsel implicitly.

But the memory of that silvery light spilling from the Véritéscope still lingered in her mind. Penelope remembered the curious sensation that had crept up her spine as its shadows danced across the makeshift screen, mesmerizing her with their sway. She had to find out how Gold's invention had cast such a spell.

"I take on board your concerns," Penelope said, her voice softening as it did whenever she tried to wheedle a favor, "but I don't think they should prevent us from agreeing to this venture. Monty has set his heart on taking a starring role in the production and we wouldn't want to disappoint our leading man. We can ill afford anymore of his theatrical flounces that might give the game away."

Wigram raised a skeptical eyebrow. "Be that as it may, Penelope, I still think we should press for changes to the contract. As it stands the only clause we requested that has made it through unscathed is the one guaranteeing Montgomery Flinch final approval of the script."

Shaking her head, Penelope picked up the pen that was resting next to the sheaf of legal papers.

"That's the only one that really matters," she replied.

Turning the pages of the contract, she reached the final page where the space for a signature was set. With a flourish, she penned the name that was renowned across the literary world, the most famous author in Britain: *Montgomery Flinch.*

"We have to give Mr. Gold his chance to bring this story to the screen."

With a tut, Wigram gathered up the agreement, shaking his head at Penelope's impetuousness. "It's your story," he replied, "but a contract like this is not one to be entered into lightly. The spectacle of the screening was impressive, I grant you, but I really think we should find out more about the Alchemical Moving Picture Company. Are we even certain they have the resources to bring this film to fruition?"

He beckoned for Alfie, who had been watching their exchange from over the proofs of the magazine's latest edition. The printer's assistant bounded over with an eager smile on his face, his excitement obvious at the prospect of the *Penny Dreadful* joining the glamorous world of the cinematograph.

"I'd like you to deliver this contract," Wigram instructed him, placing the paperwork in Alfie's hand, "to the offices of the Alchemical Moving Picture Company. Inform Mr. Gold that we will require a countersigned copy of the agreement by return of post."

As Alfie nodded his head, Penelope rose to her feet.

"I'm coming with you," she said.

As Penelope reached for her parasol, her guardian turned to stare at her quizzically.

"Don't worry, William, I won't be making any revisions to the contract behind your back," she reassured him. "I just thought another visit to the home of the Alchemical Moving Picture Company might give me the chance to find out more about Mr. Gold's bona fides. As you say, it's best to make sure that he has the means to make this film before we hand over the contract."

Unfurling her parasol in anticipation of the sunshine outside, she stepped toward the door.

"Come on, Alfie," she said, tossing her hair back with a swish that would grace any moving picture show. "Let's go to Flicker Alley."

"So the new-fangled camera that this Gold feller's invented actually works, then?" Alfie asked as they squeezed past the mounds of cinematographic equipment littering the hall. "You could see the pictures moving as well as hear the sounds?"

Penelope nodded as she stepped over a crate filled with film reels, the titles of the humdrum scenes contained within chalked on the tins: *Feeding the Pigeons, Hanging out the Clothes, The Arrival of a Train.* Brushing past a broken projector, its innards spilling out, she led Alfie toward the staircase. Behind them, the landlady's suspicious gaze followed their path, still uneasy at this constant stream of shady characters and theatrical types her newest tenants were bringing to her door.

"It was like nothing I had ever seen before," Penelope told Alfie as the two of them climbed the stairs. She struggled to find the words that could convey the strange spell the film had cast on her. "It seemed so much more real than that flickering picture show we saw at the fair. It was as though I was looking through a window into another world."

A broad grin broke across Alfie's face. "It sounds like *The Daughter of Darkness* will put *A Phantasmagoria of Fear* to shame, then," he declared. "They'll be queuing all the way up Oxford Street to see it."

Reaching the top of the stairs, they started down the gloom-ridden corridor. Alfie peered through the frosted panes of each door that they passed. He turned toward Penelope as they reached the office of the Alchemical Moving Picture Company.

"Do you think you can wangle me a look at it?" he asked with a wistful look in his eyes. "I'd love to see a talking-picture show."

Penelope paused, her hand poised ready to knock. She hadn't admitted to Alfie that this was the real reason she'd come here today—the chance to see that magical light spring forth from the Vériétéscope again. All she needed to do was persuade Mr. Gold to show off his invention and, with the signed contract in her pocket, she didn't think that would be too much of a problem.

"I'll do my best," she replied with a smile.

Through the frosted glass, the faint glow of gaslight could be seen, but Penelope noted that this time there were no raised voices to accompany their arrival. She rapped politely on the door and then heard the answering scrape of a chair being pushed back. The sound of timid footsteps scurried toward the door and then, with a squeak, it was pulled open a crack to reveal the anxious face of Miss Mottram, Gold's faithful secretary.

She blinked as she peered into the gloom, seeing first Penelope and then Alfie standing by her shoulder. An audible sigh of relief escaped from her lips.

"It's Mr. Flinch's niece, isn't it—Miss Tredwell?" Miss Mottram ventured, craning her head to see if anyone else was lurking there in the shadows. "But I don't believe I've met your companion."

"This is Mr. Alfred Albarn," Penelope replied with a twinkling smile. "He's one of my uncle's legal advisors at the *Penny Dreadful*."

Behind her, she heard a snort of laughter, which Alfie immediately tried to disguise by clearing his throat.

"Pleased to meet you," he spluttered, offering Miss Mottram his ink-stained hand. "I've come straight from the offices of the *Penny Dreadful* with instructions from Mr. Flinch himself. May we come in?"

A flustered look came over the secretary's face, but the power of Montgomery Flinch's name won through.

"Please do," she replied and, pulling open the door, she ushered them inside.

The office was just as Penelope remembered it. The peeling posters pasted to the walls, the stiff-backed chair behind the secretary's desk, its surface piled high with letters and papers, the stale odor of gas hanging in the air like a cloud. But the leather upholstery of the armchair in the corner of the room sat empty. There was no sign of Edward Gold.

"Is Mr. Gold here today?" she asked as Miss Mottram closed the door with a click.

The secretary turned and shook her head. "I'm afraid Mr. Gold is away this week, scouting locations," she replied, her fingers worrying at a loose thread on the sleeve of her blouse. "I don't expect him back until Monday at the earliest. Was it a pressing matter you needed to discuss with him?"

Penelope couldn't hide the disappointment that fell across her face. She stuttered as she tried to find the words that would unlock the door to the screening room.

"I—we—I mean, my uncle wanted me to take another look at the scene from *The Daughter of Darkness*," Penelope replied. She fixed a beguiling smile to her face. "Would that be possible?"

Miss Mottram frowned. "I'm sorry, but Mr. Gold has taken the Véritéscope with him on location. The camera and projector are one of a kind. There's no way of screening the cinematograph reel for you without it. Please give my apologies to your uncle."

Penelope sighed. There would be no chance today to delve deeper into the mystery of the Véritéscope's mesmeric power. With a tight smile of understanding, she rested her hand on the secretary's desk while Alfie reached into his jacket pocket to draw out the contract.

"Mr. Flinch also tasked me to deliver this," he began.

As Alfie spoke, Penelope let her gaze drift

over the chaos of the secretary's desk. Amid the invoices for film stock, lighting hire, and demands for unpaid bills, a handwritten letter caught her eye, its spidery scrawl written in a foreign hand.

Vous avez volé mon invention, assassiné mes rêves, et trahi l'amitié que nous entretenions. Vos actes vous exposent comme vrai charlatan. Ces menaces vides que vous avez lancées contre moi ne m'effraient pas; au contraire, c'est vous qui ne comprenez pas les dangers auxquels vous vous exposez…

Penelope's schoolgirl French was rudimentary at best, the lessons she'd spent with her governess had mostly seen her reading aloud from Henry James's *The Turn of the Screw* while her teacher listened aghast to the gothic tale. However, she recognized a few words of vocabulary from her barely thumbed French dictionary:

Stolen…Murdered…Betrayed…

One word in particular jumped out at her from the page, its meaning needing no translation:

Invention…

Her thoughts immediately returned to the Véritéscope. What manner of nefarious goings-on was being suggested here? Her curiosity piqued, Penelope leaned forward to take a closer look at the letter. At the top of the page was an address, No. 5, Leicester House, New Lisle Street, Soho, but before Penelope could attempt to translate any further, a shrill squeak of excitement turned her head.

Miss Mottram was clutching the signed contract, her eyes sparkling with delight.

"This is fantastic news," she trilled. "As soon as I read Mr. Flinch's story, I felt as though I was born to play the part of the daughter of darkness."

Penelope stared at her, askance. Although she had seen the scene with her own eyes, Penelope still struggled to square the shy figure of the secretary with the frosty heroine she had conjured on the screen. "So Mr. Gold is going to cast you in the picture?"

Turning toward Penelope, Miss Mottram blushed. "Oh yes," she replied with a timid smile. "Edward has told me he's going to make me a star."

VII

"Where are we going?" Alfie asked as Penelope turned left off the Charing Cross Road. The sun was still high in the sky, but on this side street, the buildings gave them some welcome shade. "This isn't the way back to the office. If I don't get those printer's proofs checked this afternoon, Mr. Wigram will have my guts for garters."

"Don't worry," Penelope replied, her long skirt swishing as she strode confidently on. "We're just taking a little detour. There's something I want to find out."

Intrigued, Alfie hurried to keep up. All thoughts of the work waiting for him back at the *Penny Dreadful* quickly faded away as the tone of Penelope's voice held the prospect of adventure.

The street was lined with shop fronts, much more modest in character than those of the Charing Cross Road. From their open doorways came the mingling smells of fruit and fresh pastries, the sound of tinkling bells, and the thud of a butcher's knife. But what caught Penelope's eye were the signs written across each shop front: *Charcuterie Parisienne, Libraire Cosmopolite, Blanchisserie Francaise...*

It was as though she had stepped onto the streets of Paris rather than the London she knew. As Penelope gazed up at the signs, Alfie turned toward her with a questioning look.

"So, what exactly is it you want to find out in Little France?"

That was the name given to this part of London. *Le Petit France*—the Soho streets where thousands of French men and women who had traveled across the Channel in search of better lives had settled. Here, the shops, restaurants, and even the dancing clubs all had a distinctly Continental style. Some said you could walk the length of Little France without ever hearing an English voice.

As Penelope turned on to New Lisle Street, she tried to get her thoughts in order. How could she explain to Alfie the hunch that had brought her here?

"I caught a glimpse of a letter at the film company's office," she began. "It was written in French, but I think it was about Mr. Gold's Véritéscope. It seemed to be accusing the filmmaker of several terrible crimes and I want to make sure that these claims are unfounded."

"And how are we going to do that?" Alfie asked

as Penelope glanced up at the building they were approaching. Beneath a brick parapet, the broken and boarded-up windows gave the grand house a dilapidated air. The inscription on the founding stone above the entrance read:

LEICESTER HOUSE
NEW LISLE STREET
MDCCXCI

The front door of the building was slightly ajar, a handwritten sign fixed to the peeling green paint stated: *Rooms to Let.*

"By visiting the person who wrote the letter," Penelope replied.

Lining the pavement outside the run-down boarding house was the usual assortment of idlers: scruffy young men in their shirtsleeves who eyed Penelope and Alfie suspiciously as they approached the door. One of the men, an ugly-faced fellow with a roguish moustache, muttered something to his companions as Penelope passed, his words greeted by a chorus of guffaws.

As Alfie stepped protectively by her side, Penelope kept her head held high, unswayed by the men's intimidating manner. She was determined to follow her hunch wherever this would take her. Coming to a halt outside the entrance, she peered through the gap where the door had been left ajar.

Inside, she could see a gloomy hallway with

rooms branching off to the left and to the right, and beyond these a narrow staircase reached up to the next floor. The pattern of the floor tiles had long been worn away by muddy shoes, while the dingy walls were redolent of tobacco, the faded wallpaper dating from at least the century before. There was no sign of anybody at all.

Emboldened by this, Penelope pushed open the door and, with a nod toward Alfie, led him inside. As she stepped over the threshold, Penelope wrinkled her nose with disdain. The boarding house smell was even stronger now: a heady brew of cigarette smoke, bad breath, and sewers.

"I don't reckon much to this feller's lodgings," Alfie said, puckering his face in distaste. "Are you sure this is the right place?"

Penelope nodded. "Room number five," she replied. "That's what the letter said."

They walked down the hall, the soles of their shoes sticking to the grubby tiles. Outside in the street they'd left behind a hot summer's day, but here in the gloom Penelope almost felt a chill. The doors to each of the rooms they passed were almost alike, the same peeling white paint and scuffed door handles; the only difference being the room numbers screwed into place.

Penelope stopped in front of a door bearing a crooked number five. As she raised her hand to knock, a sober thought finally caught up with her. Who was she going to find behind this door? The mysterious workings of the Véritéscope intrigued her and her glimpse of the letter had held out the tantalizing prospect of finding out more about this strange invention. But the letter had mentioned murder too. Could there be a killer waiting on the other side?

There was only one way to find out. Taking a deep breath, Penelope rapped smartly on the door. Her knock echoed in the corridor, but no answering sound came from within.

Alfie fidgeted impatiently by her side. The adventure he had hoped for was turning out to be rather a disappointment; hanging around in a shabby boarding house was a far cry from tailing crooked Bedlam guards. As the seconds wore on without any answer, he turned to Penelope with a sigh. "Whoever wrote that letter's not here," he said. "Come on, let's get back to the *Penny Dreadful* before Mr. Wigram sends out a search party."

Penelope frowned. The mystery that had brought her here still nagged away at her brain. If she could just take a look inside this room, then maybe she could find some answers. Her fingers closed around the door handle.

Watching, Alfie hissed in alarm. "Penny!"

The door opened with a creak to reveal an empty room. With a daring grin, Penelope glanced across at Alfie. "I'll only be a minute," she told him. "I just need to find out who sent that letter."

Before Alfie could utter a word of protest,

Penelope crept over the threshold and into the room. With an anguished expression on his face, Alfie glanced down the hallway to check that the coast was still clear, then quickly followed Penelope inside. As the door closed behind them with a click, Penelope took stock of her surroundings.

The only source of light came from a small window on the far wall, the sunlight outside veiled by dark calico curtains. The same florid wallpaper that adorned the hallway had spread like a fungus into this room, while the carpet underfoot was threadbare and stained. The few furnishings there were had seen better days: a sagging mattress resting on an iron-framed bedstead, a half-round table, a chest, and a chair.

Propped on the table was an array of knick-knacks: a cracked shaving mirror and straight razor, a vase of dried flowers and a stuffed squirrel mounted on a plinth. But Penelope's gaze was immediately drawn to the apparatus standing in the center of the room. Mounted on a tripod was a boxlike device, its small wooden frame filled with folding leather bellows that extended like a concertina until they ended in a round brass lens. The back of the camera was hidden beneath a black sheet that hung down like a shroud.

"Looks like the feller's a photographer," Alfie said, glancing nervously around the room. "Maybe that's how he knows Mr. Gold."

Penelope stepped toward the camera. With its

brass fittings and mahogany frame, it reminded her of the Véritéscope, even though this device didn't have the film reel you would expect to see in a cinematograph. The camera's lens was pointing toward the table, the objects left there creating a strange still life.

As Alfie silently fretted, Penelope ducked her head beneath the black cloth to take a closer look at the camera. The material fell over her shoulders, enveloping her in a musty embrace. Penelope sniffed, trying to ignore the unpleasant odor, and then pressed her eye to the viewfinder.

At first, her view was blurred as though some kind of gauze was pressed against the camera lens. But as she shifted position to try and make sense of the smeary shapes she could see, the picture suddenly sharpened into focus.

Through the viewfinder she could see the vase on the table, the delicate bloom of its dried flowers providing a splash of color against the drab wallpaper. Next to this, the mounted squirrel fixed her with a beady gaze, its paws outstretched as they reached for a nut that was no longer there. The long shadow cast by the stuffed animal reached up the wall, frozen forever in an imitation of life. Then the shadows of its paws twitched; the unexpected movement so swift that Penelope couldn't believe her eyes. She stepped back in shock, the black cloth falling from her shoulders as she suddenly straightened.

"Did you see that?" she gasped, staring at the spot where the stuffed squirrel stood.

The animal was frozen in the same posture as before; its shadow now still. No hint of a movement could be seen.

"What do you mean?" Alfie asked, his brow furrowing in confusion.

But before Penelope had a chance to explain, she heard the creak of the door opening and then the sound of a sudden exclamation.

"*Mon Dieu!*"

Standing framed in the doorway was an angry-looking man. His eyes blazed behind half-moon glasses as he stepped into the room. Penelope recognized his cropped dark hair and sharp-cornered beard immediately. It was the man she had seen storming from the offices of the Alchemical Moving Picture Company only days before.

"*Les voleurs,*" he spat, advancing on Alfie with a snarl.

As Alfie backed away, the man snatched up the razor from the table, brandishing it before him like a knife. Penelope looked on in horror, torn between the urge to escape and the need to rescue her friend. The space between Alfie and the man was narrowing with every second as Alfie backed into the corner of the room.

"Stop," she cried. "We're not thieves. I just want to know who you are."

The man turned toward Penelope, his dark eyes narrowing as they fixed on her face.

"You know who I am," he snarled, his words smeared with a thick French accent. "That's why that filmmaking thief has sent you to steal what is mine. Well, it's not going to work this time."

With a swish of his blade, he turned back toward Alfie with a murderous intent. Trapped, the printer's assistant called out with a desperate plea.

"Penny!"

Next to her, the camera squatted on its tripod. All thoughts of the strange shadow she had glimpsed through its lens were for a moment forgotten as Penelope struggled to wrench the box free.

"Wait!" she shouted. "Is this what you think we came for?"

Seeing the camera in her hands, the man stopped in his tracks.

"Give it to me," he snapped.

"Let my friend go," Penelope replied, her face set in an implacable expression. "Otherwise I'll take care of this."

The man sneered as he watched Penelope struggling to keep her grip on the camera, its cumbersome weight heavy in her hands.

"You won't get very far carrying that."

"Maybe not," Penelope replied, hefting the camera from one hand to the next, "but I can smash it to smithereens."

The camera wobbled precariously and the man's face darkened with the sudden realization that Penelope meant what she said.

"Now drop the razor and let us go."

Behind his gold-rimmed glasses, the man's eyes blazed with rage. For a moment, he held Penelope's gaze as if challenging her to go through with her threat, then his fingers twitched and the razor fell to the carpet.

"Get out."

Keeping his eyes fixed on the camera, the man watched as Penelope slowly backed away to the door, Alfie hurrying to her side. As they reached the threshold, the man raised his hand in warning.

"The camera," he reminded her.

Penelope looked down at the unwieldy box in her hands. The camera lens stared back at her, an inscrutable eye jutting from the dulled luster of its brass mounting.

"Catch," she said.

With a heave of her arms, she launched the device toward the Frenchman. As he dived to save the camera with an anguished howl, Penelope grabbed hold of Alfie's arm.

"Run!"

They fled, their footsteps clattering down the hall as behind them the man let fly a volley of unintelligible curses. Alfie barged the front door open, Penelope hurrying close behind, not allowing the swish of her long skirt to slow her for a second.

Outside on the street, the sun beat down, the few passers-by walking at a stately pace, but Penelope and Alfie didn't stop running until they reached the Charing Cross Road.

Panting, Alfie turned toward Penelope, a wry smile curling the corners of his lips. "I think you've found out all you needed to know about the person who sent that letter," he told her through halting breaths. "The man's a maniac."

Still trying to catch her own breath, Penelope nodded her head. She couldn't shake the image of the razor blade glinting in the Frenchman's hand. Despite the warmth of the day, Penelope shivered. They'd been lucky to get out of there alive.

She glanced at her watch, the time nearing a quarter to two. This was a mystery that would have to wait for another day.

"Let's get back to the *Penny Dreadful*," she said decisively, sweeping back her disheveled hair into a semblance of style. "We've got a magazine to publish."

VIII

Penelope stared at the cover proof laid out on her desk, the artwork for the August edition finally in place. Beneath the familiar masthead of the *Penny Dreadful*, its gothic letters emblazoned in red, the figure of a man blundered through the heart of a forest. He was dressed in his nightclothes, the unfastened belt from his checked dressing gown trailing in the leaves while he raised his arm to ward off the flailing branches that scratched at his face. Across the bottom of the cover, the contents line proclaimed:

Featuring
"A GREEN DREAM OF DEATH"
by Montgomery Flinch
and thirteen more tales of terror

Penelope leaned closer to inspect the illustration. With his dark whiskers and close-clipped beard, the

65

man in the picture reminded her of the mysterious Frenchman. It had been over a week since she and Alfie had fled from the boarding house on New Lisle Street, his angry curses echoing in their ears. Any thoughts of returning there had been stymied by her memory of the glinting razor blade.

But this hadn't stopped Penelope from investigating the mystery further. The letter had spoken of a stolen invention, so her first port of call had been to the elegant buildings of the patent office, just off Chancery Lane. Here she had searched for any patent application for the Véritéscope, but the clerks could find no record of this. It had been the same story when she had checked the lists of registered companies, with no records filed for the fledgling Alchemical Moving Picture Company. And of Mr. Gold himself, they had heard no word apart from a countersigned copy of the contract returned by post a few days ago.

Penelope tapped her fingers against the desk. So far everywhere that she had looked to try to find out more about Gold and his curious invention she had only turned up blank pages. There was something that she was missing here...

Her musings were interrupted by the rattle of the door handle. Penelope looked up from the cover proof to see the front door of the office flung open with a theatrical flourish. With the sunlight streaming in behind him, Monty bounded into the office, his voice booming out in greeting.

"What a glorious day it is today!" he proclaimed, a broad smile lighting up his face. "The London streets look almost elegant in the sunshine. It is a pity I have to bid them good-bye."

Monty was dressed in a striped flannel blazer with smartly pressed trousers cut from the same cloth. Beneath this blazer, Monty's shirt was unbuttoned at the neck, his summertime ensemble completed by a straw boater set at a jaunty angle. He looked as though he was dressed for a seafront promenade rather than the streets of the city.

"Are you off on your holidays, Monty?" Alfie asked, looking up from the layouts Mr. Wigram had just placed on his desk. Next to him, the lawyer's frown deepened as his stern gaze took in Monty's garb.

"I don't think we've agreed any period of leave for you, Mr. Maples," Wigram began. "If you remember, you need to be available at a moment's notice for when the Alchemical Moving Picture Company begins their filming of *The Daughter of Darkness*."

"Don't worry," Monty replied with a grin. "I'm ready to go. My case is packed, I have the script, and the hansom cab outside is waiting to take me to the station. I just came to wish you all a fond farewell."

He raised his straw boater in a valedictory salute, but before he could turn to the door, Penelope was already on her feet.

"What do you mean?" she demanded, a note of

indignation rising in her voice. "I haven't seen any film script yet."

Nonplussed, Monty plucked a letter from his blazer pocket and handed it to Penelope.

"It arrived earlier this week," he told her. "When we met with Mr. Gold, he took the liberty of asking me for the address of my club so that we could stay in touch."

Casting her eyes over the letter, Penelope felt her sense of fury start to grow.

Dear Mr. Flinch,

I have the pleasure of enclosing the script for the cinematographic adaptation of your tale, The Daughter of Darkness. I trust you will find this to your satisfaction.

I am currently making the final preparations for filming and will be in touch shortly to confirm your travel arrangements.

I look forward to commencing our collaboration.

Yours sincerely,
Mr. Edward Gold

Seeing the storm clouds gather across Penelope's brow, Monty reached out to rest a conciliatory hand on her shoulder.

"You have no need to worry, my dear," he reassured her. "I've read it from cover to cover. The script is sensational. Some might say it even improves on your tale."

With a glowering look, Penelope shook Monty's hand from her shoulder. She turned toward her guardian, who was watching the scene with a shrewd eye.

"Can he even do this?" she demanded. "The agreement we signed was supposed to give me final approval of the script!"

Wigram shook his head with a sigh.

"The agreement gives *Montgomery Flinch* the final say," the lawyer corrected her. "We can hardly blame Mr. Gold for not knowing exactly who that is."

Fuming at her own carelessness, Penelope turned back toward Monty, who had started to edge toward the door.

"And where do you think you're going?" she asked pointedly.

"My hansom cab is waiting," Monty protested. "I need to get to Paddington Station by three. I have a train to catch."

Behind her pale green eyes, Penelope's thoughts raced. There was only one way that she'd get to the bottom of this mystery. "Tell the cab driver he'll have to wait a little longer," she told Monty. "First, I need to pack. I'm coming with you."

The carriage bounced along the rutted track, Penelope clinging to the rail of the trap as the driver sat on the box seat in front of them, his hands gripping the horses' reins. Next to her, Monty was slowly turning a bilious shade of green as the cab lurched forward again. His straw boater had been blown from his head several miles back, lost to the winds whipping in from the moor.

The evening sun lurked just above the horizon, throwing long shadows across the heather-strewn wilderness. Scattered stumps of stone dotted the vast landscape, ancient reminders of those who had walked there thousands of years before. The carriage was climbing toward one of these cairns, a windswept huddle of rocks stark against the skyline. Above this outcrop, a buzzard wheeled, searching for its prey as the light started to fade.

Penelope shivered. She could scarce believe that only a few hours before she had been sitting behind her desk at the *Penny Dreadful*. Now, as the forbidding moor stretched in every direction she could see, civilization seemed a long way away.

It had taken all of her powers of persuasion to convince Mr. Wigram that she should accompany Monty on this trip. At first, her guardian had been adamant that with the *Penny Dreadful* due to go to press in less than a week's time, and Monty a far from reliable chaperone, it was out of the question. However, as Penelope artfully employed her wiles, reminding him of the damage that Monty could wreak to Montgomery Flinch's reputation without someone to keep him in line, her guardian had finally relented. He had immediately dispatched a telegraph to Mr. Gold informing him that Montgomery Flinch's niece would be accompanying her uncle on his visit to the film set. Then, with his features set in their sternest expression, the elderly lawyer had reminded Monty exactly what his responsibilities were.

As the actor chafed at Wigram's strict instructions, Penelope had turned toward Alfie, who met her gaze with an envious stare. "I don't suppose I can come with you?" he had asked, but Penelope could only shake her head in reply. "I wish that you could," she had told him, her mind still uneasy at this rapid turn of events. "There's something not quite right about all this. I need to keep a close eye on Mr. Gold and this strange invention of his. Don't worry, I'll send word as soon as I find out more."

Dashing to the hansom cab, Penelope and Monty had made it to Paddington Station with only seconds to spare, boarding the last express train to Plymouth. As they settled into the seats of their first-class carriage, Monty had begun to regale Penelope with his tales of theatrical life, while she had leafed through the pages of the film script. As she read, her anger grew as she saw the countless alterations Gold had made to her story. The names of people and places had been changed, scenes cut and rearranged, even her heroine hadn't escaped unscathed. According to the script, Alice Fotheringay was now named Amelia Eversholt, her father had changed from an earl to a lord and their home was Eversholt Manor. Penelope fumed. How dare Gold take such liberties?

With a frown lining her brow, Penelope had continued to turn the pages of the script as through the window the London sprawl gave way to views of rolling hills, the afternoon slowly slipping away as the train arrowed westward. She felt as though she was reading *The Daughter of Darkness* through a warped looking glass, every detail of her tale strangely twisted until the story that stared back at her was no longer her own. The centerpiece of her plot, when Oliver rescues Alice from the moors and presents her with a strange stone unearthed from the depths of her father's mine to guide her home, had now been replaced with a scene where Amelia gives the boy a gift of a precious jewel in thanks for her safe return. It made no sense. Why would Gold make such a change to her story? Soon Monty's snores filled the carriage, but Penelope read on, fueled by a quiet fury, only looking up from the last page of the script as the train pulled into Plymouth station.

There, a railway porter had hefted her hastily packed case across the platform as they changed trains to a smaller branch line. Staring from the window, Penelope had watched as the rolling green slopes of the landscape grew bleaker and wilder, the train twisting and rising as it skirted the moor before finally coming to a halt at a small wayside station at the end of the line. Waiting for them there had been this lone horse-drawn carriage, the taciturn driver sent by Mr. Gold to transport them on the last leg of their journey.

Monty's exuberance had now worn away to weariness. As the swaying trap neared the rise, he stared out across the melancholy expanse of moorland, its bracken and bramble gleaming in the light of the sinking sun.

"Are we there yet?" he moaned.

The rattle of the wheels died away as the carriage crested the rise. Penelope gasped as she looked down into the valley below. The track wound down a russet-red slope, tracing the path of a stream that sprang from behind a gray boulder, but where before only ancient stones had broken the landscape, there now stood the shapes of buildings.

A cluster of cottages sheltered in the shadow of a steeple, its four towering legs braced against the earth with what looked a giant clockwork wheel rising from the summit. Beyond the pithead lay more buildings: engine houses; pumping works; a crumbling mill, its waterwheel creaking in the wind. But where you would expect to hear the rumble and hiss of industry, the scene lay in silence, the only sound the whistle of the wind across the moor.

As the trap rattled down the track, Penelope leaned forward to tap the driver's shoulder. He half turned in his seat, his weather-beaten face creased in a craggy frown.

"Where are all the people?" she asked.

With a grunt, the driver pointed with his whip to the horizon. There, beyond the blight of the mine, lay a broad tangle of woodland. Rising above the trees, a Gothic tower was silhouetted against the skyline, bathed gold by the rays of the setting sun.

"Eversholt Manor," he replied, his broad accent almost unintelligible to Penelope's ears.

Penelope settled back in her seat, her brow furrowed in confusion. This was the name of the place in the rewritten final script. As the carriage trundled down the track, she saw the half-hidden turrets creep ever closer. The driver spurred the trap past the stone buildings that lay in the shadow of the pithead, an acrid smell rising from the ruins of the smelting house.

Monty wheezed as the driver raised his whip again, the horses straining as the track began to rise.

Loose scree tumbled from the mounds of spoil as the wheels of the carriage trundled past, gradually leaving the scene of the mine behind as they curved upward on the lane that led to the manor house. A few minutes later, they had reached the cover of the trees. The branches moaned and flailed in the rising wind, and, as he pulled his blazer more tightly around himself, Monty cast a superstitious glance into the shadows.

"This place could do with some electric lamps to light the way," he grumbled. "I don't know why we've had to come this far anyway. Surely Mr. Gold could've filmed *The Daughter of Darkness* in a London studio."

Penelope frowned. "Have you even read my story?"

Before Monty had a chance to reply, the carriage suddenly swung to the right. Bracing herself against the rail of the trap, Penelope found herself looking up a long, dark drive to where a grand house stood. As the horses trotted down the drive, Penelope stared up at the hall. It looked as though it had been hewn from the same granite that littered the moors; black towers and turrets rising up against a darkening sky. The front of the building was draped in ivy, its dark green leaves creeping around countless windows and crawling up the stone walls, but from the porch there came a faint glimmer of light.

The driver brought the carriage to a halt in front

of this entrance. As Monty swung down from his seat with a groan of relief, a tall man stepped out of the shadows to greet them.

"Good evening," said Mr. Gold, his vulpine features lit with a smile. "Welcome to Eversholt Manor."

IX

"Come in, come in," said Gold, his voice booming as he beckoned Monty and Penelope to follow him into the vast entrance hall. Mounted high along its wood-paneled walls, gas lamps were flickering into life with a hiss, as outside the last remnants of daylight slowly faded. Behind Penelope, two footmen dressed in threadbare uniforms were unloading their cases from the carriage. "Your belongings will be taken straight up to your rooms, but before you retire, let me first give you the grand tour."

As Monty hurried to follow the filmmaker, Penelope gazed around the entrance hall. From floor to ceiling, the walls were wainscoted with solid oak, the dark shade of the wood giving the grand space a somber air. A huge elk's head stared dolefully back at her from its vantage point, its sprawling antlers casting ominous shadows across the vaulted ceiling.

"I hope you'll agree, Mr. Flinch, that I have found the perfect place to set your tale," Gold continued as he led Monty across the stone-tiled floor. His arm swept along the length of the hall, the gesture taking in every aspect of its gloomy grandeur. "I knew the first time I glimpsed it that *The Daughter of Darkness* had found her home."

Monty peered nervously into the shadows. "Very impressive," he replied with a shiver, as though a sudden chill was creeping into his bones. "A little remote, perhaps..."

A broad grin spread across the filmmaker's face. "That's why this film will be true to the authenticity of the tale," he replied. "Here I can capture the wild beauty of the moors, the blighted shadows of the mine, and of course, the grand architecture of Eversholt Manor."

As Gold strode down the hall, Penelope fell into step beside Monty, listening intently as the filmmaker continued to speak.

"Of course, there are other benefits to our splendid isolation. As you've seen, there's not a town within two hours' drive of here, nothing to distract us as we work to bring your story to the cinematograph screen. Without any interruptions, we should complete the filming within a week."

Monty paled at the thought of spending a whole week trapped in this place.

"Is there not even a village nearby?" he ventured hopefully. "A country pub, perhaps?"

Gold shook his head, the corners of his smile tightening almost imperceptibly. "Not since the mine closed down," he replied, "more than a year ago. Only a few families remain, still living in the shadow of the pit."

Turning right at the end of the entrance hall, Gold led Monty and Penelope into a grand dining room. But instead of seeing a table laden with supper beneath its dusty chandelier, they were greeted instead by a scene of industrious toil. Burly men dressed in shirtsleeves were unloading boxes of cinematographic equipment, while on the opposite side of the room several women sat sewing costumes, their weather-beaten skin the same color as the moor. A handful of children were scattered at their feet, babes in arms and sullen-faced striplings, most of the older ones busily sewing buttons too.

"They were all so grateful when I offered them a chance to earn an honest wage again," said Gold, turning back to Monty with an expression of almost fraternal pride. "Though when I first invited them up to the manor house, I think most of them believed they would turn to stone if they ventured inside. I'd almost forgotten how superstitious folk are around these parts. Well, you must know that, Mr. Flinch, with the stories that you've set here."

Smiling nervously, Monty nodded his head as Penelope glanced across at the filmmaker with a peevish frown. Gold had barely acknowledged her presence since she and Monty had arrived; hardly the manners she'd expect from a gentleman.

As they walked along the length of the dining room, several of the children glanced up from their tasks. From faces that somehow seemed older than a handful of years, their stares followed Penelope's progress. Opening a set of double doors, Gold ushered her and Monty into the adjoining drawing room, the doors closing behind them with a click and shielding them from further scrutiny.

"May I ask how exactly you came to film here, Mr. Gold?" asked Penelope as her eyes took in the finery of her new surroundings. The spacious drawing room was decorated with rich drapery and furnishings of the most elegant design. Suspended on the walls were several portraits in gilt frames, each one situated beneath a painted coat of arms. A magnificent marble chimneypiece dominated the center of the room, its grate an ornate display of polished steel and burnished gold, while a large window looked out across the wilderness of the moor, its windswept trees now shrouded by the gathering darkness. "I wouldn't have expected the owner of so fine a home to have flung open their doors to a filmmaker."

For a second, Gold's eyes narrowed as if recognizing the barb in Penelope's question. Then stepping toward them both, he clapped Monty on the back.

"I see your niece is as sharp as a tack, Mr.

Flinch," Gold replied with a forced smile. "For hundreds of years, this manor house has been the ancestral home of the Eversholt family. Hundreds of acres of moorland, the village, and copper mine too, came under their command. However, when the last Lord Eversholt died without an heir, the estate was put up for sale by the Crown."

Gold glanced up at one of the portraits hanging on the wall. The painting showed the late Lord Eversholt, his imposing figure dressed in voluminous ermine robes. Only his face was uncovered, and a touch of cruelty lingered in his painted smile.

For a second, a flicker of hatred gleamed in the filmmaker's gaze. Then, dropping his eyes from the portrait, he turned again toward Monty. "The estate has languished unsold for nearly a year now and when I heard that Eversholt Manor lay empty, I knew that I had found the perfect location."

The filmmaker turned his gaze toward the window. He looked out across the landscape to where the silhouette of the pithead rose above the trees, almost lost in the gloaming. "I persuaded the solicitor in charge of the sale to allow me to film here, convincing him that this would bring a horde of prospective purchasers to his door. After all, who would not wish to live in the house where the illustrious Montgomery Flinch had set his tale?"

As Monty beamed, a frown creased Penelope's

forehead, the reason why Gold had changed the setting of her story suddenly becoming clear. But this still didn't explain all the other changes he had made.

The sound of a timid knock at the drawing-room door interrupted her thoughts.

Turning toward the door with a twirl, Gold raised his voice to a showman's bark. "Come in!"

The door squeaked open and the face of Miss Mottram peered shyly around the frame. Seeing Montgomery Flinch and his niece standing alongside her employer, she half bowed in greeting as she entered the room.

"Good evening, Mr. Flinch, Miss Tredwell," she began, her voice a little tremulous. "I'm sorry to disturb you, but Edward—I mean, Mr. Gold— asked me to bring him tomorrow's script pages as soon as they were typed." In her hand she held a loose sheaf of typeset pages. "I'll just leave these here for you, sir."

Miss Mottram carefully set the sheaf of papers down on the reading desk that was stationed next to the fireplace.

Penelope's gaze narrowed as she eyed the script. What fresh meddling had Gold inflicted upon her story?

Clearing her throat, she turned toward the filmmaker. As he glanced across at her, Penelope cast her face in an expression of wide-eyed wonder, fluttering her eyelashes as she spoke. "My uncle let me read your script on the journey down, Mr. Gold," she gushed, "and it was remarkable to see his story in the new light you have cast upon it. What a talent you have, taking his words from the pages of the *Penny Dreadful* and reimagining them for the silver screen."

Gold grinned immodestly.

"There was just one thing that I wondered," Penelope continued, a puzzled frown creeping across her features. "Why have you made so many changes? The scenes on the moor, the argument in the drawing room, even the grisly ending. None of this is as it was described in my uncle's story. Why, even the daughter of darkness herself now answers to the name of Amelia Eversholt. Are these amendments really necessary?"

At Penelope's question, a dark cloud passed across the filmmaker's face. He frowned, meeting her gaze with a glowering stare. "The most frightening tales, Miss Tredwell, are those that the audience believe to be real. *The Daughter of Darkness* may be my inspiration, but there are other stories that lurk within these walls as well. Rest assured the changes I have made all add to the truth of this tale." Beneath the lamplight, Gold's dark eyes glistened, but before Penelope could ask another question, he turned away to face Monty. "You have no objections, I trust, Mr. Flinch?"

"None at all," Monty replied blithely. "I'll leave the business of filmmaking to you, Mr. Gold, and concentrate my energies instead on bringing the character of Lord Eversholt to life."

"Excellent!" Gold exclaimed, clapping Monty on the shoulder as Penelope silently seethed. "And tomorrow you will have the chance to meet the rest of the splendid cast I have assembled, including the actress I have chosen to play the part of Amelia Eversholt."

Standing by the door, Miss Mottram's face paled as she heard these words, her lips suddenly blanching with apprehension. Penelope's thoughts slipped back to the gloom of the Flicker Alley screening room. She remembered the secretary's face gazing out from the silver screen.

"I thought that you had already cast that role," Penelope began, watching Miss Mottram's fingers whiten as they gripped the door handle. The secretary's trembling hand betrayed the emotions that her tight-lipped expression tried to hide. "In the scene that you showed us—"

Gold cut her off with a peremptory wave of his hand. "Oh, that was merely a screen test, Miss Tredwell," he replied dismissively. "A show reel to demonstrate the storytelling power of the Véritéscope. For the actual film of *The Daughter of Darkness*, I needed a new star—an actress who could capture the grace and poise of Amelia Eversholt."

With a stifled whimper, Miss Mottram fled from the room, the drawing-room door banging shut behind her. At this sound, Gold glanced over his shoulder, a flicker of irritation momentarily crossing his features. Then, with a shrug of his shoulders, he turned back to face Penelope, delivering the final words of his reply in a laudatory tone.

"I will have the pleasure of introducing Miss Vivienne Devey to you tomorrow, when we film the opening scene at the mine."

X

A pale face stared out from the carriage window, soft curls of raven hair framing her delicate features. The girl squinted nervously into the sunlight, lifting her hand to shade her gaze as she took in the scene before her.

The carriage had come to a halt close to the shadow of the pithead, the horses whinnying impatiently as the nearby waterwheel creaked in the wind. A huddle of men and children were clustered around the carriage, their faces filthy and their ragged clothes hanging off their stooped frames. Some of the youngest children looked no more than seven or eight years old, the shackles around their wrists and ankles clanking as they dragged themselves forward.

The tall figure of a man stepped down from the carriage, the collar of his shirt upstanding beneath his black frock coat, a dark red necktie knotted in a cavalier fashion around his throat. Grabbing the riding crop from his driver's hand, he snapped it with a whip crack to clear a path through the gathering throng.

"What is the meaning of this insolence?" Monty barked, his dark-eyed gaze thunderous beneath bristling eyebrows. "Get back to work at once!"

At the sight of the flashing whip, the workers closest to Monty's path shrank back in fear, but one of the oldest children was pushed by the others to the front of the throng until he was standing directly before him. Monty stared down his nose at the boy's upturned face. Beneath a mop of black hair the boy's grimy countenance somehow had a healthier glow than the sallow, frightened faces around him.

"Didn't you hear me?" the actor snapped, flexing the riding crop in his grasp. "Why has the mine fallen silent? I want to see you all back down that pit, bringing up my copper." He curled his lip into a snarl at the boy's silent defiance. "Maybe I should make an example of you, boy, to show the others what happens to any workers that slacken."

"But please, Lord Eversholt," the boy began, his quavering voice sounding strangely refined despite his threadbare clothes. "There's been a flood in one of the tunnels. I was just pulled free in time, but my friend is still trapped down there. Nobody can work until the level is pumped dry."

A look of concern flashed across Monty's face. "Which tunnel is flooded?" he demanded, as behind him in the carriage window the young girl pressed a handkerchief to her lips in horror.

"The lower main level," the boy replied. "One hundred fathoms deep. It's the tunnel that was dug out last week to search for new deposits."

At this news, Monty blew out his cheeks in relief.

"There's no need to worry, then," he said. "We leave the tunnel flooded and get back to the levels where there's still copper to be dug." He raised his voice to a pitch of stern command. "Now shut down those pumps and get back to work."

With this final order, Monty turned to return to the carriage, but before he could leave, the boy reached out and tugged at his sleeve.

"But, sir, my friend is still down there—"

Glancing down, Monty grimaced at the sight of the urchin's grubby paw on the cuff of his coat.

"How dare you!" he snarled. He drew back his arm in anger, the riding crop raised high in the air, ready to punish the boy's impertinence. But before he could strike, an anguished cry rang out from the carriage window.

"No!"

For a split-second the action froze, Monty's arm suspended in midair, then Gold's voice rang out across the scene.

"And cut!"

From her vantage point, half a dozen paces to the filmmaker's right, Penelope watched as Gold emerged from behind the Véritéscope, a broad smile breaking across his face. With one deft action, he cranked the camera's winder a final half-turn, bringing the whirring film reel hidden inside to a halt. Then he stepped away from the tripod and strode toward his leading man as Monty finally let his arm fall, the riding crop swishing harmlessly by his side. Next to him, the grubby face of the boy turned to watch Gold's approach too, his features anxious as he awaited the director's verdict.

"That was wonderful!" Gold declared as he reached the two of them. "Mr. Flinch, your performance was simply sublime. Lord Eversholt himself came alive in your every action."

Beneath their bristling brows, Monty's eyes twinkled at this praise, his haughty countenance relaxing into a grin. "Ah well, I must confide in you, Mr. Gold, that I have played many a leading role before in amateur theatricals," he replied. "As a schoolboy, my Sweeney Todd had my classmates cowering in their seats. This blue-blooded scoundrel isn't too much of a stretch after bringing that butcher to life on the stage." He waved his riding crop in the direction of the Véritéscope. "I just hope that your cinematographic device saw it all."

Monty glanced back over his shoulder at the raggedy band of men and children now standing idle, waiting for the filmmaker's next command, and then lowered his voice to a conspiratorial tone. "I'm sure that some of these fellows were blocking its view of my grand entrance when they swarmed around the carriage. Any chance we could film the scene again?"

Gold glanced down at the fob watch that hung from his waistcoat pocket. It was nearly midday. High in a cloudless sky, the sun beat down, bathing the mine in a golden light. The conditions for filming were perfect. With a nod of his head, he agreed to his star's request. "If one more take will make you happy, Mr. Flinch," he replied magnanimously, "then one more take you shall have."

Gold turned his gaze toward the boy standing by Monty's side. "And this time, James, let me hear the fear in your voice," he snapped. "You sounded as though you were asking Lord Eversholt for the time of day, not begging him to save your friend's life."

Beneath his artfully mussed hair, the young actor's face fell, the gleam of his blue eyes amid the grime suddenly dulled by disappointment.

His direction delivered, Gold turned away from James to address the assembled throng. "A five-minute break," he told them with a clap of his hands. "As soon as I've set the camera for the shot, we'll take that scene from the top."

As Gold paced a path back to the tripod, Monty slung a consolatory arm around the young actor's shoulder. The sight of it seemed oddly strange to Penelope, the villainous lord of the manor offering some kindly words of advice to one of his downtrodden workers. The rest of the extras hunkered down in the shadows of their own homes.

Penelope yawned. For the last hour she had stood here beneath the shade of her parasol, watching as Gold shaped the scene. The filmmaker had led Monty and the rest of the actors through the action countless times, twitching their strings like a puppeteer then retreating behind the lens of the Véritéscope to try and capture the spark. As Gold fussed again with his machine, threading the film reel into position, Penelope's gaze wandered across the scenery.

When she'd arrived there that morning to watch the filming begin, Mr. Gold had offered her only a cursory greeting. Fixing his eye to the camera's viewfinder, he'd waved Penelope away, telling her she could stay and watch as long as she kept out of the shot. He hadn't even taken the trouble to introduce her to the stars of her story.

Still feeling a nagging sense of annoyance at this slight, Penelope spotted the carriage. At its window, she could see the raven curls of *The Daughter of Darkness*'s leading lady, Miss Vivienne Devey. Penelope glanced across at Gold. With the door to the Véritéscope hanging ajar, the filmmaker was still fiddling with the spokes and sprockets inside. He wouldn't be ready to begin filming again for at least another five minutes. That would give her plenty of time to make her own introductions.

Unfurling her parasol, Penelope stepped toward the carriage, carefully picking her way across the loose stones on the path. At the sound of Penelope's approach, Miss Devey's gaze turned toward her. Raven curls of hair framed the actress's face, her porcelain skin flawless in its perfection. She looked only a year or so older than Penelope herself, but her green eyes glittered with what seemed like a superior air.

"Miss Devey," Penelope began, "I wondered if I might introduce myself?"

The girl stared disdainfully down at her from the carriage window. "And who exactly are you?"

Penelope's cheeks colored at the older girl's rudeness. For a second, she stumbled over her reply. "I'm the—I mean to say, I'm Penelope Tredwell," she stuttered. "You've already met my uncle—Mr. Montgomery Flinch—the author and star of this tale."

At this mention of England's most celebrated writer, Miss Devey wrinkled her nose with a sniff. "I think you will find that *I* am the star of this production," she replied curtly. "Mr. Gold has assured me of that, even though as yet I've only spoken a single line." She brushed a stray curl of hair from her forehead and then cast a dismissive glance in Penelope's direction. "I mean, it may as well be you sitting here for all the difference it would make—although we'd have to keep the camera away from your face."

Penelope's mouth fell open in shock, her already flushed cheeks turning scarlet with indignation at the older girl's insult. Before she'd had the chance to summon up a suitable reply, the sound of a boy's voice came from behind her.

"Pay no mind to Vivienne. She thinks she's the next Lillie Langtry."

Penelope turned around to be greeted by a smudgy smile. Dressed in the ragged clothes of a miner, the young actor inclined his head in greeting.

"Whereas I am the first James Denham," he said with a friendly twinkle in his eyes. "I'm very pleased to make your acquaintance, Miss Tredwell. I am a keen reader of your uncle's work and it is such a privilege to be working with him on this production."

Penelope proffered her hand in reply but then recoiled slightly as she saw James's grimy fingers reaching toward hers.

Seeing her reaction, the young actor glanced down at his hand. "Ah, I'm sorry," he apologized with a rueful grin. He brushed his hand against a threadbare trouser leg. "I had quite forgotten that I look as if I have just climbed out of that pit."

From the carriage window, there came the sound of a scornful laugh. Ignoring this, James met Penelope's gaze with a solicitous look.

"So what do you make of our performance so far, Miss Tredwell?"

Penelope took a moment to compose her reply. Her gaze flicked past James to take in the scene at the pithead: the huddling extras, men and children alike, sheltering from the pitiless sun, and Monty swishing his riding crop with a venomous swipe as he strode back toward the carriage. Every sight a twisted reflection of the story she had written.

With an almost inaudible sigh, Penelope returned her gaze to meet James's earnest stare.

"My opinion is really of no consequence," she replied. "I am sure my uncle will—"

Her sentence was interrupted by a sudden flurry of handclaps. Penelope turned to see Edward Gold emerge from behind the Véritéscope, the inscrutable stare of its camera lens returning her gaze. With a wave of his arms, the filmmaker exhorted the resting extras to rouse themselves from the shadows.

"If you could all return to your places, please," he demanded in a hectoring tone. "We have a moving picture to make here."

XI

Penelope awoke with a start. For a moment, she couldn't remember where she was, struggling to shake the blanket of dreams from her senses as she pulled herself into a sitting position. In the inky blackness the only sound she could hear was the thumping of her own heart.

Penelope strained her eyes against the gloom. Faint rays of moonlight crept around curtain edges, casting strange shadows across the scene. As her eyes adjusted to the darkness, she could see the shape of a wardrobe towering above her like a beast of prey. Next to this, the silhouette of her suitcase finally reminded her where she had rested her head after the long day filming: her room in the guest wing of Eversholt Manor.

As the frantic thrum of her heart gradually quieted, Penelope sat there in the stillness of the night, trying to work out what exactly had woken her. It was then that she heard it again:

the soft tread of footsteps upon the wooden floor. A prickle of fear crept across her skin with the realization that she wasn't alone. With trembling fingers Penelope reached for the candle on her bedside table, scrabbling for a match and striking it into life.

"Who's there?" she called out, holding the match to the candle's wick as its flame took hold. As the circle of light slowly banished the gloom, Penelope's gaze swept the room. In the broad mirror that sat upon the dressing table, she saw the pale outline of a young woman's face, her eyes staring anxiously out into the darkness. As Penelope's hand reached up to her mouth in fright, she saw her reflection do the same, a sudden smile of relief breaking across both of their faces. There was nobody else there.

But behind her nervous grin, Penelope knew that something wasn't right. An unpleasant sensation still crawled across her skin, as if something or someone was watching her even though it was plain to see that the room was empty. Moments passed in silence, and Penelope was just about to dismiss the whole thing as an attack of the night terrors when, from the window, there came a rustling sound.

Glancing up, she was startled to see the heavy curtains shiver as though moved by a breeze. Throwing back the bedclothes, Penelope snatched up the candle from her bedside table, holding this aloft as she marched toward the window and pulled the curtains back.

The window was locked shut.

Penelope shivered. Outside beneath a full moon, the moors lay still; not a whisper of a breeze could be seen as the trees slept in silence.

From the room behind her, Penelope heard a faint sigh, followed by the sound of shuffling footsteps.

"Monty, if this is your idea of a joke…"

The words died on her lips as she turned to see the room was still empty, the sound of footsteps falling upon the wooden floor where no feet could be seen. As a creeping panic seized hold of Penelope's heart, the bedroom door slowly swung ajar and she heard the soft tread of this invisible presence step into the corridor beyond.

For a second, Penelope stood there frozen, unable to believe the evidence of her own ears. But then she heard the familiar creak of footsteps descending the stairs. There was something out there.

Tightening her grip on the candlestick, Penelope followed the footsteps, the thud of her heartbeat threatening to drown out their sound. Leaving her room, she held the candle before her like a brand, its flickering flame throwing dancing shadows across her face as she walked down the corridor. The soft tread of her own steps echoed in the darkness, the chill night air bringing goose bumps to her skin.

From the landing, the grand staircase curved down to the hall below. Pausing there for a moment, Penelope strained her ears to try to make out a sound. Beneath the shadowy gaze of the portraits that lined the walls, she heard a faint creak, the footstep so light that she almost thought she had imagined it.

Then, at the bottom of the stair she glimpsed a shadowy form glide past the newel post, moving toward the doors of the dining room. Trailing her free hand down the banister, Penelope hurried down the stairs, a heady mix of adrenalin and fear driving her pursuit of this presence. Despite all the haunting stories she had written in the guise of Montgomery Flinch, Penelope didn't believe in ghosts, but this was beyond her rational understanding. She had to find out what was happening here.

Penelope reached the bottom of the staircase as the shadow disappeared through the dining room doors. The grand hall lay in darkness, its stone-tiled floor freezing beneath her bare feet. From the walls, the portraits of previous generations of Eversholts watched her as she stepped toward the dining room and, suppressing a shiver, Penelope reached for the door handle.

The dining room door squeaked open, the noise of it painfully loud. As Penelope cautiously entered the room, the flame of her candle threw a flickering light across the scene. Hanging from the dining room ceiling, the crystal chandelier sparkled and beneath this, the dining table lay silent, its handsome chairs empty and the dinner plates and cutlery long cleared away. From the open window there came the distant screech of an owl, the moorland outside bathed in a spectral light as a swooping silhouette wheeled above it in search of its prey.

Penelope's eyes searched the shadows, but every patch of darkness lay still. There was no sign of the strange presence that she had glimpsed at the foot of the stair. A flicker of doubt crossed Penelope's face. Had she imagined it? At the far end of the room a second door stood slightly ajar. If what she had seen was real, there was only one place it could have gone.

Penelope now headed toward that dark oak door, her nightgown gliding noiselessly across the floor. The flame from the candle lit her face with a golden glow; her expression was set in an inquisitive stare, her thoughts fixed on what she would find. Turning the handle, the door opened to reveal a room shrouded in gloom.

As Penelope stepped inside, the glimmering pool of candlelight illuminated dark oak bookcases, their shelves filled with countless leather-bound volumes. These books stretched into the shadows, while farther back the depths of the room still lay in darkness. Penelope could see the outlines of seats and tables, the shapes of reading desks and several easy chairs, but her gaze was drawn to the three-legged silhouette that stood alone in the center of the room: the Véritéscope.

For a moment, she stood there motionless, straining her ears against the silence. The room was filled with shadows, but all of these were static too. No flickering phantoms could be seen and the only sound that she could hear was the solemn ticking of a grandfather clock.

With her free hand, Penelope drew the collar of her nightdress more tightly round her neck, goose bumps still prickling her skin. Her gaze slowly returned to the Véritéscope and her mind flicked back to Gold's grubby backstreet office and the shadows she had seen dance across the screen. A trick of the light, Wigram had called it, but it had conjured a scene so real, she had almost forgotten herself. Perhaps that was what she had glimpsed at the bottom of the stair, some kind of optical illusion cast by the moonlight.

Setting her candle upon a nearby stand, Penelope stepped toward the camera, a sense of curiosity now creeping in where fear had lurked only moments before. The brass fittings of the cinematograph box glinted in the candlelit glow and she noticed that the small door on its side hung slightly ajar. Looking closer, she could see the film reel hidden inside, fixed into place amid a confusion of spokes and tubes. Penelope closed the door with a click, an intrigued smile creeping across her lips. Maybe she could solve at least one mystery tonight and discover how the workings of this machine created such a mesmeric effect.

Its lens was pointing toward a white sheet draped over one of the bookcases, creating a makeshift screen. Examining the camera, Penelope searched for the mechanism that would coax the device into life; her absorbed fascination leaving her blissfully ignorant of the shadowy fingers, now reaching out of the trailing darkness for her throat. Beneath the winder, Penelope's own fingers found a switch and, as she pushed this forward, the winding handle began to turn of its own accord. With a whirring sound, a silvery light sprang forth from the lens of the Vériéscope and splashed across the hanging sheet.

Behind Penelope, the shadowy fingers slowly disintegrated into motes of dust, dancing in the reflection of this ghostly light. Penelope watched as the swirling patterns on the screen slowly disappeared to reveal a familiar scene. In the shadow of the pithead, a carriage rattled to a halt. From the aerie of his box seat, the driver peered nervously at the ragged band of workers barring the track, their filthy hands raised high in a plaintive appeal.

Entranced, Penelope could feel the warmth of the sun seep from the screen, but the expressions on the faces of the men and children gathered around the carriage were cold and foreboding.

Above the creak of the waterwheel, she heard an angry shout and then, dressed in the garb of Lord Eversholt, Monty stepped down from the trap, his dark eyes blazing with a barely contained rage.

"What is the meaning of this insolence?" he barked, snatching the riding crop from the driver's hand as he forced his way through the throng. Flinching at every crack of the whip, Penelope shrank back in fear as his glowering face filled the screen. "Get back to work at once!"

Penelope wanted to flee, but the shadows on the silver screen held her spellbound. The camera had pulled back to show the huddled mass of workers, tattered clothes hanging from their haggard frames. She felt as though she was standing there among them, and she watched the scene unfold with a growing sense of dread.

A boy was pushed forward to the front of the crowd. The camera closed in on the boy's haunted gaze, his grimy countenance almost as black as his hair.

"Didn't you hear me?" Monty snapped, his face twisting into a snarl. "Why has the mine fallen silent?"

The boy stared back at him, a faint glimmer of hope still shining in his eyes. "But please, Lord Eversholt," he began. "There's been a flood in one of the tunnels."

Half holding her breath, Penelope listened intently to the boy's impassioned speech. The words ripped from the pages of *The Daughter of Darkness* were at once so familiar, yet also strangely new. As he pleaded, the image of the trapped child took shape in Penelope's mind. She could see his frightened face, alone in the darkness, dazed as the floodwaters rose to his neck. In that moment, his perilous plight seemed to her so real that Penelope almost forgot that this was a story.

On the screen, Monty turned to leave, dismissing the boy's pleas with a shrug of his broad shoulders.

"We leave the tunnel flooded," he said, raising his voice to a loud tone of command, "and get back to the levels where there's still copper to be dug. Now shut down those pumps and get back to work."

Penelope watched as the boy reached out with a desperate hand to tug at Monty's sleeve.

"But, sir, my friend is still down there—"

Monty glanced down at the boy's grubby paw, his lip curling into a snarl.

"How dare you!" he roared, raising the riding crop high in the air. As the boy cringed in anticipation of the blow to follow, Penelope couldn't stop the cry that escaped from her lips as, from the screen, a raven-haired girl called out the same.

"No!"

At this cry, the image froze, the frame slowly flickering and then fading from view as the silvery trail of light disappeared and the screen turned black. On the side of the Véritéscope, the winder whirred to a halt as the reel inside ran out with a click.

Transfixed, Penelope's gaze clung to the screen, the sheet now shrouded in darkness again. She could scarcely believe what she had seen. Every moment had seemed so real. Penelope shivered; the room was suddenly cold.

Behind her, beyond the circle of candlelight, she heard a faint rustling sound. Penelope turned, her heart thudding in her throat as from the shadows she saw a dark shape rise from the depths of an armchair. Snatching up the candle from the stand, Penelope took a faltering step forward, thrusting the flame before her like a rapier to keep this specter at bay.

But instead of a ghost, the face of a man emerged, blinking from the shadows. His ruddy features had a curious waxy sheen. As he rubbed the sleep from his red-rimmed eyes, his gaze fell upon Penelope, and he let out a low gasp of surprise.

"Amelia, is that really you?"

It was the filmmaker, Edward Gold, his handsome features set in a haunted frown. Penelope froze in fear as, with a heavy tread, Gold stepped toward her, reaching out with a trembling hand.

"It worked," he said, his voice little more than a cracked whisper. "It brought you back to me."

Gold's fingers brushed against Penelope's as he reached for the shimmering light. She recoiled

104

at his freezing touch, the candle slipping from her fingers and falling to the floor, its flame suddenly extinguished. In an instant, darkness surrounded them.

Penelope felt as if she had been plunged into the depths of an icy black pool. She stared into the darkness, trying to make sense of the shadows that danced before her eyes. Then the silence was broken by the sound of a sob.

"Amelia…"

Penelope turned and fled. Blundering through the shadows, she flung open the study door. Moonlight chased her silhouette as she raced across the dining room floor, not daring to glance back until she reached the grand staircase.

In the gloom of the study, Gold's shoulders shook as he slowly wound the handle on the side of the camera. The Véritéscope whirred into life, a brilliant light springing forth from its lens again, and the filmmaker stared spellbound as the shadows danced across the silver screen.

XII

"Where is that blasted girl?"

Monty rose from his armchair, the tails of his jacket flapping as he strode past dark oak bookcases. He stood foursquare in front of the wide bay window. Outside, the moors were bathed in sunlight, the russet slopes flecked with gold.

"If I find that she has left this house without my leave," Monty said, his voice taking on a stern tone of warning, "she will face the full force of my fury." He rested his hand against the window frame, surveying the landscape with a malevolent eye. His gaze fell upon the distant mine, nestled in the crook of the valley. "And if she has dared to return to that place—"

"And cut!"

Monty glanced up in surprise as Gold's shout rang across the study.

"But my speech still has another two pages to run," Monty blustered. "What's the point of my learning these lines if you keep cutting me off in my prime?"

With an apologetic shake of his head, Gold looked up from the viewfinder to meet Monty's disgruntled gaze.

"I'm sorry, Mr. Flinch," he replied, his hand winding the handle on the side of the Véritéscope forward another half-turn, "but we need to press on with the story. It is time for Amelia Eversholt to take center stage."

Behind the filmmaker, the figure of Miss Devey stood primly by the study door. She was dressed in a blue silk evening gown, a summer shawl draped decorously around her shoulders, her delicate features pinched into an impatient scowl.

"At last," Vivienne muttered, her words unheard by all except Penelope standing nearby.

Penelope watched as Mr. Gold ushered Vivienne into place, positioning her in front of the grand marble fireplace, then turning back to fuss over the camera once more as he readied the Véritéscope for the next shot. Dark shadows lurked beneath his eyes, the easy smile he had worn during yesterday's filming now replaced with a tight-lipped frown.

Of last night's strange encounter, he hadn't said a word. As the company had assembled for breakfast before that day's filming began, Gold had barely afforded Penelope a second glance. Perhaps he had dismissed their meeting as some kind of nocturnal hallucination, an imaginary case of mistaken identity as the story of *The Daughter of Darkness* crept into his dreams. But something about the experience troubled her still. As she had fled up the staircase, back to the safety of her room, she could have sworn that she heard footsteps following her, but when she turned to look nobody was there.

The sound of a sudden hiss in her ear made Penelope jump.

"The nerve of the man!"

Monty appeared at Penelope's shoulder with a glowering look on his face. "One would almost think that Mr. Gold has forgotten that it's the face of Montgomery Flinch that the audiences will be flocking to see."

Penelope arched her eyebrow. "I think you'll find that it's Montgomery Flinch's stories that the public are eager for," she replied.

With a distracted flutter of his fingers, Monty waved her objection away. "But the audience will expect more than just a mere glimpse of my performance. The queues for my recent readings at the Royal Albert Hall stretched halfway across Hyde Park."

Penelope rolled her eyes at Monty's melo-dramatic claim.

"After all, my dear," the actor continued, puffing out his chest, "did you not think that my performance just now would have kept the audience on the edge of their seats?"

Over Monty's shoulder, rows of leather-bound volumes stretched along a bookcase that only hours earlier had been hidden behind a sheet. Her thoughts drifted back to the scene she had seen played out on that screen, the flickering enchantment of light almost making her believe that she was really there. Somehow Gold's machine held the key to this mystery, but how could she find out more when the filmmaker watched the Véritéscope like a hawk, even sleeping by its side it seemed.

Behind her green eyes, another memory stirred. She had seen a camera much like the Véritéscope before. The image of the shabby rented room in Little France swam into focus in her mind. She remembered the boxlike camera, its lens fixed on a still life of dried flowers and a stuffed squirrel mounted on a plinth; the strange trick of the light that had made it seem as if the squirrel's shadow had come to life.

But Leicester House was over one hundred and fifty miles away. There was no chance to investigate further while she was trapped here. There was only one person who could help her now. Penelope glanced up at Monty, the actor frowning as he waited for her to acclaim his performance.

"I need you to send a telegram for me," she said.

Monty's frown turned into a scowl. "Of course," he harrumphed, glancing past Penelope to the spot where Vivienne was rehearsing the scene. "Playing a messenger boy might be the only chance I have to act again today if Miss Devey cannot remember her lines."

Behind Penelope, Miss Mottram stepped forward, a sheaf of script pages flapping in her hand as she hurried toward Vivienne. Snatching these from her without a word of thanks, the young actress turned away to study her lines.

"Could I just have a few moments, please," she demanded.

As a hush fell over the study, Monty rolled his eyes in exasperation while Penelope quickly scribbled her message. Folding the paper, she pressed this into his hand.

"This telegram is to be delivered to the offices of the *Penny Dreadful*," she instructed him. "For the attention of Mr. Alfred Albarn."

XIII

With his back pressed against the trunk of the tree, Professor Archibald stared up in horror at the inhuman creatures that were descending from its branches. Through the mists that still clung to the forest, he could just make out their devilish grins; more like imps of the night than any living thing. As the professor clutched at his heart in fear, the creature closest to him unfurled its claws with a slavering hiss. "So you've come to join us at last, my dear professor."

Raising his head from the page, Alfie pushed the magazine proofs across his desk with a shudder. This latest tale of Penelope's was proving to be her most terrifying yet. At the bottom of the page, beneath an illustration of a monstrous face peering through a canopy of leaves, the last line of copy held out the promise of more thrills to come.

Read the final installment of
Montgomery Flinch's spine-tingling serial
"A GREEN DREAM OF DEATH"
in the September edition of the *Penny Dreadful*.

Running his fingers through his messy thatch of blond hair, Alfie let out a frustrated sigh. How long would he have to wait until he could find out what happened next? He glanced across to Penelope's empty desk, the piles of papers and proofs there left untouched since she had disappeared with Monty into the depths of Devon. He would have given up a week's wages for the chance to accompany Penelope on this trip, anything for the opportunity to see the magic of the moving pictures up close. His head filled with dreams of the cinematograph screen: the lights and the cameras, the action and excitement. Maybe he would even have gotten the chance to appear in front of the Véritéscope himself...

A knock at the office door interrupted Alfie's daydream—probably another delivery of proofs for him to check. Shaking his head, he pushed back his chair and hurried to the door. As he opened it, he saw a messenger boy dressed in a navy blue uniform standing on the doorstep, a yellow envelope held in his hand. From beneath his pillbox hat, the boy stared quizzically at Alfie, the printer's assistant only a year or so older than him at most.

"Telegram for Mr. Alfred Albarn," he declared.

With a puzzled nod, Alfie accepted the envelope, the messenger boy tipping his hat in thanks before hurrying down the steps to where his bicycle was waiting below. Closing the door behind him, Alfie tore the envelope open and slid out the telegram. On the sepia postcard was a typed message stuck on in white strips of paper, the sender's name and location revealed at the top of the page:

POST OFFICE TELEGRAPHS
FROM:
MISS PENELOPE TREDWELL, STOKE EVERSHOLT, DEVON
SOMETHING STRANGE ABOUT GOLD'S CAMERA STOP
GO BACK TO NEW LISLE STREET STOP
FIND OUT MORE FROM THE FRENCHMAN STOP
BE CAREFUL STOP
DON'T TELL WIGRAM STOP

From his desk at the back of the office, Wigram raised an inquisitive eyebrow.

"News from Penelope?" he asked.

A faint flicker of anxiety passed across Alfie's eyes.

"Er, yes," he stuttered in reply. "Just a brief telegram to say that they arrived safely. Nothing at all to worry about."

Before Wigram could ask to see the telegram, Alfie slipped it into his pocket and sank back behind his desk, his mind now whirring with questions.

The elderly lawyer sighed, deep creases furrowing his brow as he stared at the piles of papers and proofs left on Penelope's desk.

"I wish we could say the same," he grumbled. "The deadline for the next edition will soon be upon us and I don't know how we will get the magazine ready in time without Penelope here. I knew I should have stopped her from making this foolhardy trip. I blame Mr. Maples for filling her head with all his stories of the glamour of the stage."

But Alfie was only half listening, his mind still preoccupied by Penelope's appeal for help. His thoughts flashed back to the rundown boarding house on New Lisle Street, remembering how they had both sneaked into the rented room there. He could picture the camera standing on its tripod, the only thing of any worth in that threadbare room. Then, with a shiver, he recalled the wild-eyed Frenchman wielding a razor blade. It had only been thanks to Penelope's quick thinking that they'd been able to get out of there alive. And now she wanted him to go back.

Something strange about Gold's camera, the telegram said. But how did Penelope think that madman could help her? Alfie was torn between the beckoning mystery and the fear of what might be lying in wait for him if he returned to Leicester House. He weighed the dangers in his mind, then set his features in an expression of fresh resolve. Penelope wouldn't have asked him to investigate if it wasn't important.

Rising from his chair, Alfie reached up to grab his jacket from the coat stand as Wigram glanced up in surprise.

"Going somewhere?"

Before the question had even left the lawyer's lips, Alfie was already halfway toward the door.

"I just have to pop out for a little while," he called back over his shoulder. "There's something that Penelope wants me to check at the library— research for her new story, I think."

And as the lawyer's features furrowed into a frown once again, Alfie was out of the door. As it shut behind him with a slam, he hurried down the steps, the midday sunshine already baking the busy pavement below. Turning left, he headed for the Strand and, as he left the shadows of the office behind, Alfie couldn't stop an excited smile from creeping across his lips. Now it was his turn to play the detective.

As Alfie stood outside the door, a crooked number five fixed to its peeling paint, the last traces of his excitement melted away. He glanced nervously down the hall, making sure of the quickest escape route before he dared raise his hand to knock. Swallowing hard, he rapped his knuckles against the door and heard the sound of heavy footsteps crossing the room in reply. As the door swung open, Alfie stepped back in surprise as, instead of the expected figure of the Frenchman, he was confronted by the gargantuan form of a middle-aged woman.

"What do you want?" she barked, her bare arms folded across a barrel chest. Standing in the doorway, she seemed to loom as large as the house itself and appeared to be just as dilapidated. Tufts of hair sprouted like weeds from places where no respectable lady would have willingly let them take root, while her sharp eyes inspected Alfie with disdain.

"Good afternoon, madam," Alfie began, trying to hide the nervous tremor in his voice. "Could I possibly speak to the person who rents this room?"

"I'd like to speak to him too," the woman spat in reply. "Find out where he's got to with my twenty-six shillings—that's the two weeks rent that he owes me. He just lit up and left in the dead of the night, stealing a set of my best bedding into the bargain as well. Damned Frenchies—you can't trust them with anything."

Peering past the landlady's ample frame, Alfie could see that the room was even emptier than when he was last here; the mattress on the iron bedstead now bare. There was no sign of a camera or even a suitcase, the Frenchman's few possessions now gone too.

"What do you want with him, anyway?" the woman inquired, her eyes narrowing with suspicion. "You're not one of his *friends*, are you?"

Alfie swiftly shook his head.

"I just need to ask him a few questions. I don't suppose you know where he might have gone?"

The landlady sniffed, the sound of this making a rattling noise.

"Probably back where he came from," she replied. "Working on the fairground with the rest of those vagabonds who have sullied my door of late. They're all smiles and promises at first, but then when the money runs out they sneak off back to the lowlife of the fair." The woman stooped to pluck a tattered sheaf of handbills from where they were wedged to fill a crack in the doorframe. With a scandalized tut, she thrust these into Alfie's hand. "I mean, look at what the man did—it's hardly a respectable occupation, is it?"

Raising an eyebrow, Alfie glanced down at the paper in his hand and saw the ghostly portrait of a young woman staring back at him. She was dressed in an evening gown that looked like it belonged to the last century, her bare shoulders half turned away from the camera, with long dark curls cascading over them. On the faded handbill, her figure seemed almost translucent, as though worn through by time or neglect, but something in her shadowy gaze sent a chill down Alfie's spine. Glancing away, he read the boldly lettered text that lay beneath the photograph.

Gold & Prince Pictures

"BRINGING THE SHADOWS OF THE PAST TO LIFE"

Extraordinary Portraits of your Dearly Departed Special arrangements for photographing families and children

Prices from 5 Shillings

FIND US AT THE FAIR

"And if you find that thief Jacques Le Prince," the landlady growled, "tell him that I want that money he owes me *and* my bleeding bedding back."

With that she slammed the door in Alfie's face, dust falling from its lintel onto his shoes as he stood there deep in thought. He hadn't found the Frenchman, but at least he had a lead: a name, Jacques Le Prince, and an idea of where he could find him. Stuffing the tattered flyer into his pocket, Alfie turned to leave, a smile slowly spreading across his lips. It was time to go to the fair.

XIV

Standing at the far end of the study, Penelope watched as Gold prepared the scene. The filmmaker motioned for Vivienne to take a step forward, and stooped to fix his eye to the viewfinder, checking that the actress was captured in its frame. The blue silk of her evening gown shimmered beneath the gaslight, and a nervous blush colored Miss Devey's cheeks as she waited for the camera to roll. Facing her, Monty sat behind a broad oak desk, impatience marking his features as he fixed the Véritéscope with a glowering stare.

For a machine he claimed to have invented, Gold's grasp of the camera's mechanics seemed rather limited. This last shot of the day had taken an age to set up; Monty's thoughts were already turning toward dinner and a stiff glass of port as the filmmaker prodded at the controls. Finally satisfied, Gold took hold of the camera's winder.

"The camera is ready," he declared, as he fixed his eye to the viewfinder again, then cranked the Véritéscope into life. "Action!"

In response, Monty's dark eyes blazed with fury beneath his bristling eyebrows. He glared up at Vivienne. "How dare you defy me in this way?"

In the guise of Lord Eversholt, Monty's face had taken on a beastly aspect, his whiskers encroaching wolfishly over his cheeks while his mouth twisted into a snarl.

"I shall expect nothing but insubordination from those wretches now that my own daughter has set such an example," he continued. "This is my house, these are my lands, and that is my copper mine to run as I see fit—without any interference from the likes of you, my girl!"

Spittle flecked his lips as Monty banged his fist down on the desk, the ring on his finger scratching its oak veneer. Watching on, Penelope felt a strange prickling sensation crawl across her skin. Dark shadows fell across Monty's features, a trace of real malice in his gaze as he worked himself to new heights of anger.

"I will be obeyed!" he roared.

Standing firm in the face of this tirade, Vivienne held her head high. Dark tresses of hair framed her porcelain features, and there was a frightened look in her emerald eyes, but a glimmer of defiance lurked there too.

"But, Father," she protested, "it was my

Christian duty to speak. That poor boy could have drowned in the depths of your mine."

"And his family would've been grateful," Monty snapped. "One less mouth around the table for them to feed."

He rose from behind his desk, his imposing frame towering above Vivienne as he stepped toward her. "And your duty, my girl, is to obey your father's every command. The money I have spent on your education—nursemaids, governesses, visiting masters—and all they have managed to raise for me is an insolent whelp. I am only glad that your mother never lived to see your temerity."

Vivienne clenched her slender fingers into fists, playing the part of Amelia to perfection as she addressed Monty in a tremulous tone. "If Mother could have seen the way you treat those poor children down at the pit, she would have died of shame anyway."

In reply, Monty's face turned puce with fury. As the gas lamps flickered, he raised his hand high, the shadow thrown across the wall quivering with an uncontrolled rage. As her own face filled with fear, Vivienne froze, waiting for Gold to call out and bring the scene to a close. But the cry of "Cut!" never came and the shadow swooped down with a venomous strike.

CRACK!

The sound of the slap reverberated around the room. At the far end of the study, Penelope gasped in shock, almost feeling the sting of the blow herself. Standing next to her, Miss Mottram paled. Only moments before, she had been silently mouthing Vivienne's words, but now the script pages shook in her hands.

Silence fell over the study like a shroud; the only sound that could be heard was the faint whir of the Véritéscope. Gold was still hunched over the camera, his eye pressed to the viewfinder as he remorselessly turned the winder.

With tears pricking her eyes, Miss Devey stared up at Monty in shock. Dark shadows still haunted the actor's gaze as Vivienne raised a trembling hand to her cheek, the crimson mark there branding her deathly pale features.

"You hit me!" she wailed.

Her cry seemed to rouse Monty from the spell that he was under. He stared down at Vivienne as if seeing her for the first time.

The porcelain beauty of the young actress's face was now a tear-stained mask of misery, her shoulders heaving with every sob. Monty glanced down at his open palm, the skin stung red by the force of the blow. He slowly shook his head, confusion clouding his features.

"I'm so sorry," he stuttered. "I don't quite know what came over me."

Vivienne turned to face the camera. Dark rivers of mascara streaked her blotchy features, the crimson welt on her cheek already starting to shine as she sniffed back a sniveling wail. "He hit me!" she shrieked, the shock in her voice now transformed into a shrill pitch of outrage. Blubbering sobs punctuated her every word. "That wasn't in the script!"

As Monty looked on dumbfounded, the whirring noise of the Vérítéscope came to a halt with a click. Straightening up, Gold emerged from behind the camera lens, his face grim. Stepping toward his leading lady, he drew a handkerchief from his pocket and offered it to her with a consoling hand. Still trembling, Vivienne pressed it to her eyes, staring up at Gold through her tears.

"He hit me," she repeated, her voice now as small as a child's.

Gold nodded in reply, the dark shadows beneath his eyes giving his face a haunted expression.

"I know what he did," he said, his low voice laced with certainty. "I remember it all like it was yesterday. I'm afraid that your suffering is the price we have to pay to bring the truth into the light. The shadows of the past must walk again."

Vivienne stared at him in horror.

"Now if you would kindly attend to your makeup," Gold continued, turning back toward the Vérítéscope. "The picture show must go on."

For a moment, Vivienne stood there frozen. A giddying whirl of emotions flashed across her face—shock, confusion, and fear—before her features finally settled into an expression of ungovernable fury.

"No!" With a stamp of her foot, Vivienne flung the handkerchief at the retreating figure of the filmmaker.

"I refuse to be a part of this horror show," she cried. "You said you were going to make me a star, but you've let him treat me like some common serving girl. The man's a monster! I will not stay for another minute in this beastly place."

Flinging back her hair, Vivienne gathered up the skirts of her gown, sweeping them before her as she flounced across the room. "I'm going back to London," she declared. "There are a host of West End shows where my talents will shine more brightly than in this tawdry production."

Standing by the Vériténscope, his hand resting protectively on its casing, Gold watched her leave. His gaze followed Vivienne as she swept past Penelope, still speechless at what she had seen. As the young actress reached the door to the study, only the mouselike figure of Miss Mottram stood in her path. With a rather unladylike shove, Vivienne pushed past the secretary, causing the pages of her script to fall to the floor. Miss Mottram quickly stooped, scrabbling to pick these up as Miss Devey disappeared through the open door. *The Daughter of Darkness* had lost its star.

Gold frowned, his fingers tapping out a staccato rhythm against the side of the camera. Monty turned to address the director, his head hung low in shame.

"Perhaps if I went after her," he began in a faltering voice. "If I could just explain how the emotion of the scene overcame me. Apologize for my brutish behavior…"

Gold held up a hand to bring Monty's remorseful confession to a close.

"You have nothing to apologize for," he replied in a tone that brooked no quarrel. "Your performance could not be faulted. Staring through the viewfinder, I could see Lord Eversholt himself where you now stand."

Gold's dark eyes glittered with an unshakable conviction. "This moving picture show must make the audience believe," he continued. "The truth must be told."

Lifting his eyes, Monty stared back at the filmmaker, a puzzled expression creeping across his already troubled face. "But surely without Miss Devey there can be no film?"

In answer, Gold turned toward the rear of the study. There, Penelope and Miss Mottram still waited. He stepped toward them, his dark-eyed stare flicking across each face in turn.

"We already have the perfect replacement for Miss Devey," Gold explained. "A young lady who is blessed with the same graceful demeanor as Amelia Eversholt herself. Somebody who knows the story of *The Daughter of Darkness* better than any of us here. Except, of course, for yourself, Mr. Flinch."

Clutching the script, Miss Mottram blushed with delight, a hopeful smile straying across her lips. The pages of the script fluttered nervously in her grasp, dreams of stardom shining in her eyes once again. Almost holding her breath, she watched as Gold stepped toward her, ready at last to make good on his promise.

But the filmmaker came to a halt five steps too soon. He stood directly in front of Penelope, his eyes roving over her figure like a sculptor sizing up a raw piece of clay. She shifted uncomfortably beneath his gaze, while Miss Mottram looked on perplexed, her smile starting to curdle at the corners of her mouth.

"This is our new daughter of darkness," Gold pronounced. He reached up to brush a stray strand of hair from Penelope's face, the icy touch of his fingers instantly transporting her mind back to the shadows of the night. "Amelia…"

A shiver ran down Penelope's spine. But before she had the chance to reply, a shrill scream rent the air.

"How dare you!" Miss Mottram shrieked, flinging the pages of her script in the filmmaker's direction. "I will not stay here to be so insulted twice!"

As Penelope looked on aghast, the expression on Gold's face remained unmoved. He turned toward his secretary, Miss Mottram's features now contorted with anger.

"Please arrange for Amelia's costumes to be taken to Miss Tredwell's room," he instructed her. "We shall begin filming again tomorrow."

With a final shriek of rage, Miss Mottram turned on her heel, following the path taken by Miss Devey. Storming from the room, she slammed the study door behind her, the sound echoing through the manor house.

Seemingly unperturbed, Gold turned back to face Penelope. There was mystery in his shadowy features and, leaning forward, he dropped his voice to a whisper meant for her alone.

"Don't worry, my dear," he said with a chilling smile upon his lips. "Your story will be told."

XV

Standing in front of the full-length mirror, Penelope inspected herself with a critical eye. She smoothed the silken material over her shoulders, the collar of her evening gown, half a size too small, rubbing at her skin. The dress she was wearing had been cut for the frame of Miss Devey, but with the actress returning to London in the morning, her costumes had now been delivered to Penelope's room. She glanced down at the array of clothes left in a heap on her bed, a riot of colors illuminated by candlelight. Skirts and ball gowns, blouses and shawls: the clothes that would help her bring Amelia to life when she stepped in front of the camera tomorrow.

Penelope shook her head, the thought of this filling her with dread. The fact that she was now the star of this moving picture show still seemed beyond belief, but when Gold had fixed her with his piercing stare she had felt unable to refuse.

Your story will be told, the filmmaker had said. She shuddered.

Her thoughts returned again to the strange events that had unfolded that evening. After Vivienne and Miss Mottram's dramatic exits, Monty had retired early, too ashamed by his behavior to even stay for dinner. It had been left to Penelope and the young actor, James Denham, to join Edward Gold in the dining room. There, they had listened respectfully as the filmmaker outlined his plans for the next day's filming, the atmosphere as frigid as the plates of cold meat they were served. But as the meal dragged on, Gold became more garrulous with each glass of wine that he drank, his conversation taking a slightly sinister turn.

"With this film, I will take my revenge," he had slurred, waving his wine glass at the portrait of Lord Eversholt. "The wrong that was done can finally be put right." James and Penelope had exchanged puzzled glances, both of them confused by the director's cryptic comments. Eventually, to their relief, the last course was served and, finishing it, they had hurried from the dining room, leaving Gold grumbling into the bottom of his wine glass.

Penelope frowned. What on earth had Gold meant? With a sigh, she picked up the script from her bedside table, resigned to rehearsing her first scene before she slept that night. Staring into the mirror, she addressed her own reflection:

"My name is Amelia Eversholt and this is my

story—a tragic tale of murder, betrayal, and revenge."

As she spoke the words aloud, Penelope caught a glimpse of a second face in the mirror, the shadowy features of a girl hovering at her shoulder. With a sudden gasp, she spun around in alarm. But in the shadows that lurked behind her, nobody could be seen.

A strange unearthly sensation gripped Penelope as she peered around the room. The candle's flame flickered and the shadows thickened, as though some unseen presence was trying to make itself known. At the very edge of her hearing she could just make out a soft murmuring sound, the whisper of a heartbeat next to her own.

With a mounting sense of dread, Penelope turned back to face the mirror, her heart thumping in her chest as she stared at her own reflection. She watched in disbelief as a second face emerged from the shadows again. It was the face of a girl, not much older than Penelope herself. But where Penelope's features were blanched with fear, the girl's face was wreathed in shadows; soft curls of hair framing her ethereal features like pale wisps of mist. She was dressed in a gray evening gown, a black velvet ribbon tied high around her neck.

As Penelope stared at the girl in the looking glass, it appeared to her that she could almost see through the girl's body; the image of her evening gown shifting to reveal the door beyond. An icy prickle crept across Penelope's skin as, with eyes that glittered like diamonds in the gloom, the girl fixed her with a beseeching stare. She opened her mouth to speak, but no sound came, and then with a sigh that rustled the curtains, she turned to leave.

As Penelope stood there transfixed, the shadowy figure of the girl stepped toward the door. She moved with a curious gliding motion, as if her footsteps almost skimmed the floor. Glancing back over her shoulder, the girl beckoned for Penelope to follow her and then disappeared through the solid oak door.

With her heart thumping in her chest, Penelope turned to obey; the pages of her script fluttering to the floor as she stepped toward the door, almost unable to believe what she had seen. As she turned the handle, the heavy door opened with a creak. Outside, the corridor lay in darkness, but as she stepped from her room, Penelope could just make out the shadowy form of the girl ahead of her in the gloom, gliding down the passageway as though the floor was made out of water.

Penelope hurried to keep up, the sound of her own footsteps painfully loud. At the end of the long corridor stood the outline of another door, almost lost in the darkness. The wraithlike figure of the girl paused in front of this and with an agitated gesture, signaled for Penelope to hurry. Then, turning back toward the door, she melted through the frame as though it wasn't even there.

Penelope gasped. She tried turning the handle, only to hear the rattle of the lock hold firm. Standing there in the darkness, a flurry of thoughts rushed through her brain as she tried to make sense of what she had just seen. As a shiver crept down her spine, Penelope couldn't discount the thought that some supernatural hand was at work here. Then, on the other side of the door, she heard an ominous creaking sound.

Ghost or not, she had to find out what lay inside. Pulling out her hairpin, Penelope bent to the keyhole. There was more than one way to unlock a door. Using the trick that Alfie had shown her when he'd locked the keys inside the office, she straightened the hairpin and then slid it inside the lock. Carefully turning the hairpin, she felt it catch against the pins of the lock in turn, each one clicking into place as the hairpin rotated. With a final twist, she felt the lock spring open and, turning the handle, Penelope opened the door.

The room was pitch-black; a darkness more complete than even the corridor's murky gloom. Penelope cursed her impulsiveness, wishing now that she had picked up the lighted candle from her table. She took a faltering step forward, straining her eyes against the shadows that crowded the room.

Heavy curtains were drawn across the window, but faint glimmers of moonlight crept around their edges. Steeling her nerves, Penelope stepped across the darkened room, the half-glimpsed shapes of shadows looming out at her. Reaching the curtains, she drew them back with a flourish, the full moon hanging in the sky casting a spectral light across the scene.

Penelope took in her surroundings with an inquisitive eye. A stout chest of drawers stood in one corner, a simple brass bedstead in another, while a washstand, wardrobe, and dressing table made up the rest of the furniture in the room. The bedstead was covered with a plain white counterpane, pulled tight over the pillows and sheets; no sign that anyone had slept there that night. The room was empty, but as a cold sweat crept across her skin, Penelope knew that she wasn't alone.

As if to prove her right, a creaking sound came from the corner of the room. Turning toward it, Penelope saw the top drawer of the oak chest slowly slide open as if of its own accord. As she watched, mesmerized by the impossibility of what she was seeing, a framed photograph set atop the cabinet teetered at its edge. As the drawer juddered to a halt, the photograph tipped forward and fell, Penelope rushing forward to grab it before it hit the floor.

With an anxious glance around her, she placed the picture frame back on top of the dresser. Near to it lay a copper candlestick with matches in its broad tray and, reaching for these with a trembling hand, Penelope struck a light. As the candle's flame shimmered, she caught sight of the photograph in the frame and let out a low gasp.

The faded picture showed the face of a girl, dark curls of hair framing her sad-eyed stare. It was the girl she had glimpsed in the shadows—the ghostly presence who had brought her to this place. As Penelope stared at the photograph, its sepia tones glowing gold in the candlelit glow, the chest of drawers shuddered and, glancing down, she saw the drawer pulled out again by an invisible hand.

Without thinking, she reached down to push the drawer back before its contents spilled out over the floor. But even as she pressed hard against it, bringing all her weight to bear, some supernatural force seemed to hold the drawer open. Staring down in disbelief, Penelope saw this same invisible hand begin to peel back the layers of folded sheets and pillowcases arranged there. It was as though it was searching for something, peeling back the bedclothes until the bottom of the drawer lay almost bare. Then Penelope saw it, a brownish bundle of papers tied together with a black ribbon, half-hidden beneath a folded pillowcase.

She hesitated, not wanting to risk the wrath of this unseen presence. But the drawer now lay still. Whatever supernatural force was at work here, it seemed satisfied that it had her attention. This was something she was meant to see.

Reaching into the drawer, Penelope carefully

unknotted the ribbon, lifting the uppermost of the papers out from the dresser. In the candlelight she could see letters, postcards and photographs—a secret store of memories that for some reason had been hidden away. Bending her head more closely to the first of the letters, Penelope began to read.

No. 4, Hartshorne Alley, Pimlico, London
Sunday, 31 August 1879

Dear Amelia,

I must beg your forgiveness for not writing sooner, but I feared the consequences if this letter reached your father's eyes. Although I have been forced to leave Stoke Eversholt, my concern for your safety remains undimmed by the distance now between us. The scars that I bear from the beating your father gave to me are nothing compared to the pain I glimpsed in your eyes. I cannot express my anger at the cruel treatment he has shown you and am only sorry that your kindness could be so shamefully misconstrued.

I pray night and day for your speedy recovery and, as I seek my fortune in London, I only hope that it will be in my power one day to return to right this great wrong.

Your sincere friend,
Edward

As Penelope finished reading the letter, she sensed the presence of another standing by her side. Out of the corner of her eye, she glimpsed the shadowy form of the girl, her hand reaching out toward the drawer again. Glancing down, Penelope saw a tear-shaped stone, jet-black in color, threaded upon the black ribbon that she had just untied. But beneath this stone lay a postcard-sized portrait, the face of a young man staring back at her from a faded photograph.

As she looked at this picture, Penelope felt a frisson of recognition. It was the face of the filmmaker—Edward Gold—pictured here in younger days. A pencil moustache was perched on top of his upper lip, his youthful features pinched into a nervous smile.

Shaking her head, Penelope turned toward the shadow by her side; countless questions swirling around her mind. But before she had the chance to speak, she heard the sound of heavy footsteps in the corridor outside. Penelope hurriedly swept the pile of papers back into the drawer, sliding it shut as the door handle rattled behind her.

In the candlelight, she saw the face of Edward Gold, his lined features set in a suspicious frown.

"What on earth are you doing in here?"

Penelope glanced back toward her shadow in

search of a reply, but the girl was gone. She turned to face Gold, the filmmaker's face darkening as his gaze took in the framed portrait set on the dresser behind her. Somehow he was caught up in the secrets that had been hidden there, and Penelope instinctively knew that she couldn't risk telling him the truth.

"I'm so sorry," she replied, stifling a yawn as she reached up to rub her eyes. "I think I must have been sleepwalking."

XVI

Penelope sheltered in the lee of the stone, the tall gray boulder providing her with some welcome respite from the wind that whipped across the moor. Above her head, the sky was a darkening slate, clouds creeping across the horizon and veiling the russet slopes of the valley that lay before her from view. A growing chill was in the air as evening slipped toward night.

Behind her, there came the sound of a curse. Gold was hunched over the Véritéscope once again. The three feet of its tripod were hidden in the undergrowth, sunk beneath the bracken and brambles that carpeted this lonely part of the moor. With a furrowed brow, Gold was peering inside the machine, trying to work out which element in its mysterious workings was responsible for this latest delay.

Penelope leaned back against the boulder, taking this moment's break to try to make sense

139

of the strange events that had brought her to this place. A soft mist was starting to descend from the clouds, dimming the rays of the already sinking sun. If Gold wasn't able to get the camera working quickly, there would soon be no light left to film by. Beyond the mists lay the gothic silhouette of Eversholt Manor, its towers and turrets marking the spot where that day's filming had begun.

Dressed in Vivienne's cast-off costume, Penelope had stood in the study, nerves coiling in the pit of her stomach as Gold turned the camera toward her. Then, pressing his eye to its viewfinder, he had uttered the word that had changed everything.

"Action!"

As the film rolled, Penelope had felt a strange sensation crawl across her skin, the same unearthly feeling that she had felt last night as the shadowy girl appeared by her side. As she began to speak the lines of the script, she heard the whisper of the same words breathed in her ear.

"My name is Amelia Eversholt and this is my story—a tragic tale of murder, betrayal, and revenge."

Out of the corner of her eye, she glimpsed the pale features of the girl, hanging in the air like mist, and the words dried on Penelope's lips. She stared into the Véritéscope lens in mute appeal. Couldn't Gold see her too? As her silence filled the room, the filmmaker raised his eye from the viewfinder and fixed Penelope with an exasperated glare.

"Cut!"

As quickly as she had come, the shadow was gone, leaving Penelope shaking her head in puzzlement as the camera whir faded into silence. But there had been no time to try and make sense of any of this as Gold thrust the pages of the script into her hand.

"Try to get it right, Miss Tredwell," he snapped. "Perhaps if you slept more soundly at night then you wouldn't forget your lines."

With that, he hurried back to the camera, waiting impatiently for Penelope to compose herself before he turned its winding handle again. In a daze, Penelope had stumbled through the script, the scene passing by in a blur before Gold swept her onto the next. From the manor house to the mine itself, Penelope had stepped through the pages of the story, sensing the shadowy presence by her side growing stronger with every word that she said. Now as darkness crept across the valley, the final scene left to be filmed today was Amelia's desperate attempt to escape from her father's clutches, fleeing from the manor house and out across the moor.

Penelope shivered. Something about this story haunted her, more so than when she had first shaped its plot for the pages of the *Penny Dreadful*. It was no longer Montgomery Flinch's tale; Gold's changes to the script meant that it now belonged to Amelia Eversholt. But who exactly was she?

"Miss Tredwell!"

Gold's voice cut through the gloom, the last glimmers of sunlight fading fast. Peering around the edge of the stone, Penelope saw the filmmaker standing over the Véritéscope, his hand poised on the winder.

"Move to your mark," he barked, unable to hide his impatience. "This is the final shot of the day."

With her cheeks coloring at his effrontery, Penelope followed Gold's order, tramping across the bracken until she reached the path that wound across the moor. Turning back to face the camera, she squinted into shadows, the creeping mists now hiding even Gold himself from sight, but his voice still came to her on the wind.

"Action!"

At the sound of this word, an icy shiver ran down her spine as, from the shadows, the ghostly figure of the girl emerged. She seemed more real now than when Penelope had last glimpsed her, whirls of mist clinging to her clothes as she stepped along the path. The last gleam of sunset was fading from the sky, leaving the two of them alone with the night.

"Who are you?" Penelope asked, fighting to keep the tremor from her voice.

The girl lifted her head to fix Penelope with a plaintive stare, a glittering darkness shining in her eyes. "Amelia," she replied.

A sudden fear filled Penelope's veins; her only

instinct a desperate desire to flee from this phantom conjured from the pages of her story. Gathering up her skirts, Penelope blundered past the ghost girl, scrambling down the path as the fog enveloped her like a shroud. Suddenly lost in a world of shadows, she felt clammy fingers of mist pluck at her skin. Stumbling over tussocks of heather and gorse, she tried to keep to the path, but her foot snagged against a tree root, pitching her forward into the darkness.

Flinging out her arms to save herself, Penelope felt her hands sink into soft heather, brambles scratching at her skin as she rolled down a quickening slope. She cried out in alarm, her momentum sending her pitching forward until she sprawled in a heap at the bottom of the bank.

For a moment, she lay there dazed, staring up into the shadows and seeing only stars. Then, through the gloom, she saw a faint glimmer of light moving to and fro, the shadow of a boy walking along the treacherous path, a shimmering lantern held in his hand. Penelope opened her mouth to call out for help, but then the words dried on her lips as she saw the ghostly figure of the girl step forward to greet him.

As he reached her, the boy lifted his lantern, its light falling across his features to reveal the face of the young actor, James Denham. His pale blue eyes shone with concern.

"Are you lost, miss?" he asked.

From the shadows, Penelope watched as Amelia's ghost nodded her head, her figure almost translucent as the light from his lantern threw a protective circle around them both.

"I've been lost for such a long time," she replied, a faint tremor in her voice as James recoiled in fear. "I can only thank the Lord that you found me."

As she lay slumped at the bottom of the bank, Penelope felt a dizzy lightness steal into her mind, the peculiar sensation growing stronger with every word that the girl spoke.

"These moors are dangerous, miss." James stuttered out his line, scarcely able to believe his eyes. "You should be back at Eversholt Manor."

The ghost girl nodded, the pale beauty of her features almost worn through by the light.

"Take me home," she told him.

The young actor blanched beneath the lantern light. There was fear in his eyes as her wraithlike hand stole toward his own. Then from across the moor came a harsh snapping sound, like a spring or a coil breaking, and with a cry that quickly faded into a sigh, Amelia melted into the mist, disappearing completely.

For a moment, James stood there frozen, staring into the shadows where Amelia had stood; then the young actor jumped in alarm as out of the darkness, Penelope rose unsteadily to her feet. He glanced down at the muddied ruin of her dress, her dark hair disheveled from the effects of the fall. The two of them stared at each other, but before either could speak, Gold marched from his vantage point nearby on the moor, his face flushed with excitement.

"That was the best one yet," he told them, his eyes shining brightly in the lantern light. "If only the camera hadn't broken down…" His eyes swept from James to where Penelope was standing in the shadows. Taking in her piteous state with a frown, Gold narrowed his gaze. "We must try again tomorrow."

XVII

"Playing the part of this monster is driving me to distraction!"

His face flushed with concern, Monty leaned forward across the dining room table and jabbed his fork into an open dish. Brandishing the speared sausage like a blubbery finger, he pointed it at Penelope with a flourish.

"This blasted story of yours will be the end of me, Penelope. I swear that Lord Eversholt's villainy is poisoning my mind. I've not felt this way since I understudied Macbeth at the Garrick, back in eighteen ninety-five."

Grease dripped from the undercooked sausage, staining the linen tablecloth below, before Monty stuffed it into his mouth with an angry grunt.

From the other side of the table, Penelope glanced up at the actor, the dark rings beneath her pale green eyes telling the story of her own anxiety. The breakfast plate in front of her lay untouched, a solitary piece of toast left forgotten on the side. After a sleepless night, her mind was still filled with thoughts of the girl who had haunted the evening's filming: Amelia's shadow finally stepping into the light.

"So what are we going to do?" Monty demanded, shards of half-eaten sausage spluttering from his mouth as he stared at her expectantly.

Penelope's brow wrinkled in confusion.

"Do about what?" she asked.

Now it was Monty's turn to frown.

"About getting out of this ghastly place!" he exclaimed. "We must convince Mr. Gold to shelve his plans for this moving picture show and return to London without delay. I promise that I will throw myself into the role of Montgomery Flinch once more—anything to escape from this shadow that plagues me."

Penelope stared back at Monty in surprise, torn between her own misgivings and her desire to solve the mystery that lay here. "But the contract has been signed," she began. "The *Penny Dreadful* has promised Mr. Gold that he alone can make the picture show of this tale. We can't just leave."

Monty scowled. "You would say that," he snapped. "Especially seeing as how Gold has seen fit to make you the star of this production. I hadn't been aware before now, Penelope, that your ambitions lay in the direction of the stage. In fact your guardian, Mr. Wigram, has always made it quite plain to me that he prefers you to stay out of the limelight." Monty rose to his feet and fixed Penelope with a sharp-eyed stare. "I wonder what he would say if he knew of your starring role."

Penelope paled. She knew exactly what her guardian would say. Mr. Wigram had always impressed upon her the risk of her real identity being discovered if she stepped too close to the flame of Montgomery Flinch's fame. The idea that a mere girl could write the masterful tales of terror that graced the pages of the *Penny Dreadful* would be too much for the critics to bear. Montgomery Flinch's continued success depended on this secrecy.

She pressed a hand to her temple as a strange, woozy sensation swam into her mind. Gazing down at the polished silver of her breakfast plate, Penelope saw the pale reflection of Amelia Eversholt staring back at her, a shadow creeping across her brow.

As quickly as it had come the reflection disappeared, almost as if she had imagined it. Shaking her head as the dizziness passed, Penelope looked up to meet Monty's gaze with a pensive stare.

"We have to stay," she told him.

The color drained from Monty's face. For a second, he stood there in silence, swallowing hard as he considered his response. Then, with a theatrical gesture of surrender, he threw up his arms in dismay. "Fine," he snapped, turning away from the table to leave. "If you need me, I'll be in my bedchamber studying the script." Monty flounced from the room, the angry stomp of his footsteps echoing through the manor house.

A sudden feeling of weariness came over Penelope. Trying to clear her mind, she fixed her gaze on the moors that lay beyond the large bay window, taking solace in the picturesque scene. Beneath a cloudless sky, the rugged hills looked almost benign, a far cry from the treacherous heath she had braved last night. Even the ugly blight of the abandoned mine, its crumbling buildings nestled in the crook of the valley, seemed somehow softened by the sunlight.

As Penelope stared in the direction of the distant pithead, she heard the soft whisper of a voice in her ear.

I've been lost for such a long time...

Spinning around in her seat, Penelope searched in vain for the source of the voice, but only faint shadows lurked at the edge of the room. She buried her head in her hands, her fingers trembling as the faint murmuring started again.

But now I'm coming home...

Penelope pressed her fingers to her temples, trying to quiet the voice in her mind. When she crafted her tales for the pages of the *Penny Dreadful* she was used to conjuring up characters, hearing their voices inside her head as she directed their actions, but this insistent whisper made her feel like she was being possessed.

"Are you all right?"

The sound of another voice caused Penelope to glance up in surprise, the whispering suddenly silenced. She saw the face of a boy not much older than herself, his black hair neatly slicked into a side parting, while his features were composed into an expression of the upmost concern.

For a moment, Penelope couldn't place the boy's face, unused to seeing it without its customary layer of grime. Then as he walked toward her, the realization struck as she stared up into James's kindly eyes.

"I'm fine," she replied, sweeping a stray lock of hair from her face with a fretful gesture. "Just a little tired perhaps from the strain of all this filming."

The young actor held Penelope's gaze, seemingly unconvinced by her reply. She noticed for the first time the dark circles beneath his pale blue eyes, his features marked by the same haunted expression that troubled her own.

"Can you see them too?" he asked her, keeping his voice low as if fearful of being overheard. "The shadows that infest this place?"

XVIII

"I cannot escape them; they haunt me wherever I turn."

Beneath his furrowed brow, James's face seemed worn beyond his years, weariness etched into his features. Penelope gazed up at the young actor as she listened to him pour out his concerns. He had told her how the ghosts of *The Daughter of Darkness* now stalked his every scene, apparitions of Lord Eversholt and Amelia herself appearing from the shadows, even as the actors spoke their words aloud.

"Tell me," James asked, meeting Penelope's gaze with an anxious stare, "do you think I am going mad?"

She slowly shook her head. If James was mad, then she was as well, both of them plagued by the shadows that haunted this place. Some greater mystery lurked within these walls and she needed to find out what it was.

"No," Penelope replied, "I don't think that."

A faint sigh of relief escaped from James's lips as he ran a hand through his slicked-back hair.

"I've acted in countless productions, Miss Tredwell," he said, "but of all the roles that I have played, on stage and for the cinematograph screen, none have made me feel this way. When Mr. Gold turns the handle of that camera, I feel as though I am trapped—a prisoner inside your uncle's story as these specters he has conjured rise to greet me."

Penelope stared up into the boy's eyes, seeing the anguish that lurked there.

"Perhaps I should speak to your uncle," James continued. "Surely Montgomery Flinch must have some kind of explanation for the spell that his fiction has cast here…"

As his voice trailed away in despair, Penelope shook her head again.

"I think that we should seek our answers from Mr. Gold," she said. "After all, he is the man behind the camera."

Matching Penelope's stride, James hurried along the gallery, his face turned toward her as she outlined her plan.

"Mr. Gold is filming today's first scene in the library," she reminded him. "If these strange apparitions we have seen are not mere tricks of the light or products of our fevered imaginations, then he might have captured their passing with his camera. If we could just take a peek at what lies inside the Véritéscope, then perhaps we could find out more."

Outside, the morning sun was still rising in the sky, but here inside the wainscoted walls of the gallery, gloom reigned supreme. The shadowy faces of portraits stared down at them as a flicker of unease passed across James's features.

"Are you sure?" he asked. "I don't think Mr. Gold will look too kindly on that. Just remember how he treated poor Vivienne and his secretary, Miss Mottram, when they crossed his path."

With a shiver, Penelope thought back to the scene that had brought her to this point. Miss Devey's face streaked with tears while Gold had looked on with a cold-eyed stare; Miss Mottram raging against her employer's betrayal as he passed the mantle of the leading role onto Penelope herself. Gold had completed his humiliation of both ladies the very next day, returning them to London on the back of a farmer's cart, the director's own newfangled motorcar sitting idle in front of the great hall. With Vivienne by her side, Miss Mottram had tried to hold on to her decorum as the cart lurched down the drive toward the station, but her features couldn't hide her seething resentment.

At the time, Penelope had watched her leave with a puzzled frown, little understanding why Gold would treat his faithful secretary with such disdain. It was only when she returned to her room and found the note slipped beneath her door that she had started to make sense of his cruelty.

Dear Miss Tredwell,

I cannot depart from this place without leaving you this word of warning. Whilst I have been in Edward's employ I have kept my own counsel, but after the events of this last week I now feel no compulsion to hold my tongue.

There is a darkness that lurks in this place; one that I fear has infected Edward and now creeps ever closer to your uncle too. The villagers speak of the ghosts that stalk the manor house, and they refuse to work after sunset. Some even say that they have seen Lord Eversholt himself walking again on the moor. At first I thought these were the superstitions of simpleminded folk, but when Edward presses his eye to that infernal camera of his, I can almost believe that they are true.

I thought that Edward cared for me, but I see now that his only concern is for those shadows he conjures across the screen. I have tried to speak to him of my fears, but his only reply is that the truth must be told, and when I look into his eyes I no longer recognize the man who stares back at me. My meager inheritance is gone—squandered in rent on those shabby Cecil Court offices—and now my dreams of stardom have disappeared too but, please believe me, I bear you no malice for this. To be gone from this place is all that I ask for now.

When I first read your uncle's story, I believed that The Daughter of Darkness would make the actress who played her a star, but these changes that Edward has made to the tale make me fear for your safety. You are in danger here and I urge you to leave before it is too late.

Yours truly and sincerely,
Miss Ethel Mottram

Penelope pressed her hand to the pocket of her dress, feeling the outline of Miss Mottram's note there. A small part of her wished she was back behind her desk in the offices of the *Penny Dreadful*, a place where the stories that she penned stayed under her control.

Penelope and James passed beneath a painting of a young woman dressed in a gray evening gown, a black velvet ribbon tied high around her neck. Her sad-eyed stare followed their path down the corridor, neither of them noticing the nameplate fixed to the portrait frame:

THE HONORABLE MISS AMELIA EVERSHOLT
BORN 5 JUNE 1864; DIED 28 SEPTEMBER 1879

They were nearing the door to the library now and Penelope only hoped they would find the answers they were searching for within. Reaching the door, her fingers closed around the handle, pushing it open as she led the way inside.

The room lay in darkness, heavy curtains drawn across the large bay window, leaving the library shrouded in gloom. Edward Gold was nowhere to be seen.

"Maybe there's been a change of plan," James said, nervously glancing around the room.

Penelope shook her head. In the shadows she had already spotted the familiar silhouette of the tripod, Gold's peculiar camera perched atop of it. The lens of the Véritéscope was pointing straight at them, fixing her with an unblinking stare.

"This is the right place," she said.

Penelope took a step forward, the Véritéscope watching her as she approached, while James hung back near the door.

"Perhaps we should wait for Mr. Gold to arrive," he said, as Penelope ran her fingers along the camera's brass casing. "If he saw you touching that..."

Penelope scowled. From the moment she had signed Montgomery Flinch's name across the bottom of that contract, the filmmaker had been dictating her every move. Seized by the urge to make a stand at last, her fingers sought out the switch beneath the camera's winder and, pushing it forward with a click, the Véritéscope whirred into life.

As the winding handle turned, a silvery light shone from the camera lens, casting a shimmering shadow across the spines of the books lining the far wall. The vast bookcase was transformed into a cinema screen, the swirling patterns that drifted like mist across the dust jackets slowly parting to reveal the darkened moor.

Penelope heard James gasp in surprise, but her own eyes were fixed to the screen, watching as a solitary light loomed out of the gloom; the figure of a boy trudging through the mist, a glowing lantern held in his hand. Then, from out of the darkness, a second shadowy form entered the scene, her clothes wreathed in mist as she stepped forward to meet the boy.

"Are you lost, miss?" James asked, his voice crackling from the camera.

The girl nodded her head, lifting her eyes to fix him with a deathly stare.

"I've been lost for such a long time," she replied. "I can only thank the Lord that you found me."

Standing in the darkness, Penelope's temple throbbed; a strange light-headed feeling returning as she watched the ghostly figure of the girl step toward the light.

"These moors are dangerous, miss." The stuttering sound of James's voice filled the room. "You should be back at Eversholt Manor."

On the screen, the phantom reached for James's hand, his eyes filling with fear as she spoke again.

"Take me home."

At the sound of these words, the picture froze, the ghostly image of the girl flickering and then fading from view as the silvery light disappeared back into the dark eye of the Véritéscope. Unaware until that moment that she'd been holding her breath, Penelope let out a long sigh of relief.

She turned toward James, the young actor still staring spellbound at the space where the moving picture had been.

"Surely the camera cannot lie," Penelope began, her voice trembling with excitement. "She *was* there—out there on the moors. The ghost of Amelia Eversholt."

James's face was pale, his gaze still fixed staring straight ahead. "She's here," he murmured.

With a sudden shiver, Penelope realized that the winding handle was still turning. As the whirring sound of the camera whispered in her ear, she turned to see the ghostly figure of the girl emerging from the darkness of the bookcase. Penelope gasped. In the half-light, the girl's wraithlike features looked almost gray, starved of any sunlight, and as she opened her mouth to speak, Penelope felt a dizzying sensation seize hold of her mind again.

"You have brought me home," Amelia said, the whisper of her words seeming somehow to fill the room. She stepped forward again, the spines of the books lining the shelves behind her still visible through her shadowy form.

James stood there frozen, his eyes filled with fear. "What do you want?" he stuttered.

With ghostly fingers, Amelia reached up to the black ribbon tied around her neck and Penelope noticed, for the first time, the jet-black stone that was threaded there. Shaped like a tear, its obsidian surface seemed to shimmer in the gloom.

"I once gave you the gift of this stone," Amelia whispered as she stepped forward again, her feet seeming to glide across the floor. "Now you are giving me the gift of life in return. I want to thank you, Edward."

Unfastening this simple necklace, she held it out toward James with a shadowy hand. In the dimness of the library the stone shone with an unearthly light.

From her position beside the Véritéscope, Penelope stared at it transfixed. She felt as though the room was spinning, the ghostly figure of the girl growing more real with every moment that passed. Her mind whirled, this peculiar light-headedness making her feel as though she was about to faint. Penelope reached out for the camera to steady herself, her hand catching hold of the winding handle as from the corridor outside there came the sound of footsteps.

As a shadow fell across the doorway, Amelia let out a panicked cry. The hulking figure of a man loomed large in the gloom. Beneath bristling eyebrows, they caught a glimpse of the ghastly face of Lord Eversholt, his translucent features set in a snarl of rage.

Penelope felt herself falling into a swoon. As she slumped toward the floor, her fingers tightened around the camera's winder, wrenching it to a standstill. With a groaning sound, the Vériténcope juddered to a halt and, with a gasp, Lord Eversholt and Amelia melted into the darkness, their shadowy forms disappearing as if by magic.

Slumped against the tripod, Penelope shook her head; the strange dizziness slowly clearing as she stared at the empty space where Amelia Eversholt had stood.

"What the Devil's going on here?"

Edward Gold rushed into the room, his features contorted with fury as he strode toward the camera, pulling Penelope to her feet with an angry cry. "How dare you!"

Penelope winced, the man's grip around her wrist painfully strong. She cast a desperate glance past Gold's shoulder, imploring James to come to her aid. But the young actor just stood there in silence, slowly shaking his head, looking for all the world as if he had just woken from a nightmare.

Gold twisted Penelope's wrist to drag her gaze back to his. The dark shadows beneath the director's eyes gave his face a fiendish aspect.

"Where is she?" he hissed.

In her mind, Penelope could still see the image of Amelia's ghostly figure, the memory of this making her shudder, but before she could even try to answer the sound of another voice boomed across the room.

"Are you all right, Penelope?"

Penelope glanced across to see Monty standing in the doorway, his brow furrowed as he took in the sight of Gold's hand wrapped around her wrist. As Monty raised a questioning eyebrow, Gold released his grip, meeting Monty's gaze with a stern-faced stare.

"I would appreciate it if you could remind your niece, Mr. Flinch, that this equipment of mine is not some toy to be trifled with. The Véritéscope is a unique invention—a precision instrument—not the plaything of some giddy young girl."

The filmmaker brushed past Penelope to attend to his invention, carefully inspecting the camera to ensure that it hadn't been damaged in any way.

Normally Penelope would have bristled at his barb, but out of the corner of her eye she caught sight of a glint of light, some tiny object lying abandoned on the floor. Stealing forward, she reached down to pick it up, her fingers closing around a tear-shaped stone. As Gold fussed with his camera, Penelope stared down at the stone with a growing sense of disbelief. The jet-black jewel was ice-cold to the touch, its glittering darkness slowly fading to a dull glow as she held it in her palm. This was the same stone that had hung round Amelia's neck, somehow now made real.

"It is your good fortune, Miss Tredwell, that you appear to have avoided causing my invention any irrevocable harm." The sound of Gold's voice made Penelope jump in alarm. "From now on I must insist that you stay in front of the camera."

Hiding the stone in her hand, Penelope reluctantly nodded her head in reply. But behind her green eyes, the realization was growing that the mystery that lay here was darkening at every turn. With an air of disapproval, the filmmaker turned back toward Monty.

"Now, Mr. Flinch," he declared. "It is time for us to rehearse this morning's action. There are only a handful of scenes left to be filmed. Soon, the story of *The Daughter of Darkness* will reach its rightful end."

Penelope shivered at these words. She knew from the script the grisly coda Gold had penned for her tale; the final scene where Lord Eversholt would meet his comeuppance. Her blood ran cold at the thought of the horror still to come.

XIX

Alfie pushed the pile of proofs across his desk with a sigh, the thick wedge of pages covered with countless corrections for him to make. He'd be lucky to get away from the office before nightfall. Mr. Wigram's desk, with its empty chair, stared back at him reproachfully. Before he had set off for his meeting that morning, the elderly lawyer had instructed Alfie to make sure that all the printer's proofs were checked by the end of the day.

"I think you have spent quite enough time at the library helping Penelope with her research," Wigram had told him. "It's time you got down to some real work. The deadline for the September edition is almost upon us."

Alfie shook his head with a sigh. He couldn't tell Mr. Wigram that this research had involved him visiting half the fairs in London in search of Jacques Le Prince. From High Barnet to Britannia Fields, he'd searched in vain for any trace of

163

the elusive Frenchman, asking stallholders and fairground hawkers if they had heard of Gold & Prince Pictures, but all to no avail. The case of the missing Frenchman remained unresolved.

Reluctantly he turned to the next pile of paper. His detective work would have to wait for another day. But as he bent his head to his task, there came the sound of a sharp knock at the door. Grateful for this distraction, Alfie leaped to his feet, pushing back his chair and hurrying to the door. As he opened it, he saw a primly dressed woman standing on the doorstep, the handle of her parasol raised high as she prepared to knock again.

On seeing Alfie's face, the woman's eyes lit up in recognition. "Mr. Albarn," she declared in a tone almost as shrill as her expression. "Thank goodness you are here. I need to speak to you on a matter of grave urgency."

Lowering her parasol, the woman brushed past Alfie as she entered the office, leaving him standing there perplexed. Closing the door behind her, Alfie turned with a frown as he tried to work out exactly who she was.

The woman was dressed in a checked walking suit, the wide lapels of her jacket cut in a style that had last been in fashion in the previous century, while the hemline of her skirt afforded the merest glimpse of a pair of slightly plump ankles. She was standing by Alfie's desk, tapping the tip of her parasol impatiently against the floor as she waited to address him.

For a moment, Alfie was at a loss, unable to place her face. "If I can I help you in any way, miss—"

"Miss Mottram," the woman replied in as confident a squeak as she could muster. "I am—I mean to say, I *was* Mr. Edward Gold's secretary at the Alchemical Moving Picture Company. We met, Mr. Albarn, when you returned Montgomery Flinch's signed contract for the cinematographic adaptation of his story *The Daughter of Darkness*."

In an instant, Alfie remembered Miss Mottram's face; her plain features lighting up with a squeal of delight as he had handed over the contract.

"Of course," he replied, blushing slightly as he recalled too how Penelope had told Miss Mottram that he was one of Montgomery Flinch's legal advisers. "And what precisely brings you to the *Penny Dreadful* today? I trust all is well with Mr. Gold's production."

The secretary fixed him with an anxious stare. "Edward Gold has turned into a monster," she replied, every word delivered in a hushed tone of fear. "And his invention threatens to do the same to Mr. Flinch. That's why I've come here today—to warn you of the dark shadows that this moving picture has cast and beg you to help bring it to an end."

Alfie's mouth fell open in surprise. "What do you mean?"

"Since he reached Eversholt Manor and started filming *The Daughter of Darkness*, Edward has been a man transformed," Miss Mottram began. "His every kindness has turned to cruelty. I cannot tell you of the evil that haunts that place when he stands behind the Véritéscope to bring the story to life. It has even infected Montgomery Flinch himself—I have seen him strike out in a rage, reducing poor Miss Devey to tears."

Alfie shook his head in disbelief. "That's impossible, Monty wouldn't—" He caught himself just in time, cutting off his own sentence before he said too much.

Miss Mottram cast him a curious glance. "You seem to be on rather familiar terms with your employer," she replied with a sniff, "but I know what I saw, Mr. Albarn. Something wicked lies at the heart of Montgomery Flinch's tale and, with his niece, Penelope, now playing the part of the prima donna, I fear that she will be the next to fall prey to its poison."

Alfie stared back at her blankly. "The prima what?"

"The leading lady," Miss Mottram wailed, her patience finally snapping. "She has taken the role of Amelia Eversholt and is playing the part of the daughter of darkness herself."

With this final revelation, Miss Mottram burst into tears. For a moment, Alfie stood there nonplussed, staring in consternation as the young woman's shoulders heaved with every sob. Then he reached into his pocket to extract his handkerchief, offering it to her with a nervous hand. The once-white material was covered in a spider web of ink stains, but Miss Mottram accepted it without a second glance, blowing her nose with a mournful honk.

His mind racing, Alfie tried to piece together everything that she'd told him: Edward Gold turned into a monster by his own invention; Monty flying into a violent rage; and now this declaration that Penelope had taken the lead role in the production. Alfie shook his head. He remembered Penelope's scornful reaction to the picture show they had watched at the funfair. There was no way she'd have ended up starring in one.

Miss Mottram let out another sniveling sob. The woman was almost hysterical. Could he even believe a word that she said? He glanced across at Mr. Wigram's empty desk, wishing the elderly lawyer was here to listen to Miss Mottram's evidence.

"I'm very sorry," Alfie began as the former secretary's sobs finally quieted to a low sniffle, "but how do I know that you're telling me the truth? What proof do you have for these wild accusations?"

Miss Mottram stared back at him. "It is of no consequence to me whether you believe me or not, Mr. Albarn," she replied in a trembling voice. "But if you care for Mr. Flinch's well-being and the safety of Miss Tredwell, I urge you to do everything in your power to bring an end to this film."

This warning delivered, Miss Mottram turned and headed for the door. As she opened it, Alfie called out one final question.

"Then why are you telling me all this?"

Miss Mottram glanced back to reply, her red-rimmed eyes now filled with resentment. "Revenge," she said simply. "Edward has turned into a monster—more terrible even than any creature that Montgomery Flinch has ever penned. He has to be stopped."

With that, the front door closed behind her with a slam, leaving Alfie standing there alone. He shivered, her words sending a chill down his spine. He thought back to Penelope's telegram with its cryptic warning:

SOMETHING STRANGE ABOUT GOLD'S CAMERA STOP

Since then he hadn't heard a thing from her and in his heart the fear grew that what Miss Mottram had told him was true.

He glanced up at the clock on the wall. It was nearly midday. Mr. Wigram wasn't due back in the office until late that afternoon, but if Penelope was in danger he had no time to waste. He *had* to find the Frenchman and discover the secret that lay behind Gold's camera.

Grabbing his jacket, Alfie hurried to the door. Locking it behind him, he hurried down the steps, racing to leave the shadows of the office behind. He only hoped he could find Jacques Le Prince before it was too late.

XX

Alfie weaved his way through a heaving sea of people, the thickening crowd pressing in from all sides. The excited babble of sound that filled the evening air seemed to be reaching a fever pitch; the candy-striped lights of the fair flickering into life as dusk descended and the day slipped away.

"A penny a ride for the thrill of your life!"

Ignoring the bellowed entreaties of the fairground hawkers, Alfie ducked through a gap in the crowd and headed down a side alley, its stalls showcasing some of the fair's less savory exhibits:

Susie the Snake Charmer, Professor Fenwick's Flea Circus, the Wheel of Fortune and Jack Chadwick's Boxing Booth.

A cardsharper dressed in a worn velveteen jacket sat hunched over a table, a lit cheroot hanging from his lip. "Fancy trying your luck, lad?" he called out to Alfie with a wink. "Find the lady and win yourself a half crown."

Shaking his head, Alfie hurried on. It had been an arduous journey that had brought him to this place, traveling halfway across London by omnibus, tram, and underground train to reach Upper Green on the outskirts of the city just in time for the last night of the Mitcham Fair.

Back at the *Penny Dreadful*, Mr. Wigram was probably cursing his name; the pile of unread proofs on Alfie's desk getting higher with every hour that he wasted on this wild goose chase.

He peered at the stalls ahead with a frown. If he had to return to the office without finding Jacques Le Prince, there was no way that he'd be able to convince the elderly lawyer of the truth of Miss Mottram's warning. Mr. Wigram would probably think he had just taken a half day and dock him a day's wages for sure.

The noise of the fair seemed quieter here, its well-oiled patrons far fewer on the ground as these more remote attractions failed to live up to their billing. Richardson's Waxwork World of Wonders, Madame Xanadu Fortune-Teller, Tales from the East—an Exotic Magic Lantern Show. Then Alfie saw it: a shabby-looking booth at the far end of the row; its once brightly painted facade now peeling and tired, but the words above its door could still be read:

The 5 had been scored through and the number three crudely painted in its place—a desperate attempt to draw any passing trade inside.

Alfie's chest swelled with pride. Sherlock Holmes himself—God rest his soul—would've been impressed by his detective work. In a city of more than six million people, it looked like he had managed to track Jacques Le Prince down. Now it was time to find out if he had any answers.

A makeshift curtain was drawn across the entrance to the booth, but as Alfie approached this he heard the sound of a sob emanating from the interior.

"I never thought I would see her again!"

Alfie jumped back in alarm as with an anguished cry, the curtain across the door was flung open. A distinguished-looking gentleman stepped out from the photographer's booth, his silver hair and smartly clipped whiskers framing plump cheeks that were puffed out in an expression of wondrous disbelief. In his hand he clutched a large photograph and, as Alfie glanced down at

172

it, he saw the man's face staring back at him in black and white, but with the figure of a woman standing beside him.

Her expression was shrouded in shadows, her eyes meeting the camera's gaze with a coal-black stare. Below the frosty rime of her hairline, the woman's face seemed to have an ethereal appearance, her skin almost translucent. Alfie shivered as he glanced up from this ghostly image to see the man's eyes stained with tears.

"There is another world," he breathed, clutching the portrait to his chest. "Beyond this vale of tears. And now that I know that my beloved Alice is waiting for me there, I can live my life in peace until we are together again."

Wiping a tear from his eye, the man turned away, heading back toward the heart of the fair. With a sense of unease growing in the pit of his stomach, Alfie pulled back the curtain left dangling across the entrance and peered inside.

The booth was lit by two arc lamps, stationed at either side of a grubby white sheet that hung across the far wall: the missing bed linen from Leicester House discovered at last. In front of this sheet, a straight-backed chair stood ready for the next sitter, while across from the chair the figure of a man crouched behind a camera tripod. His glasses were perched halfway down his nose as he peered into the camera's interior. With an expert touch, he slid a roll of film out from the boxlike camera, placing it into the small canister that was open at his feet.

As Alfie stepped inside the booth, letting the curtain fall behind him with a swish, the man glanced in his direction.

"I will be with you in one moment," Jacques Le Prince said. "I just have to prepare the camera to shoot the next carte de visite."

He took a small penknife out of his pocket and scored open a fresh roll of film, carefully unspooling it as he threaded it into place inside the camera. With the film secured, he closed the door of the camera with a click and then rose to his feet to greet his new customer.

"Now, *monsieur*," he began. "Who is it that you wish to see? A beloved parent perhaps or maybe a long-lost friend? I am afraid there is no way of telling which spirits the camera will capture."

Jacques Le Prince held out his hand in greeting as Alfie emerged from the shadows but then curled his fingers into a fist.

"You," he hissed in disbelief. "*Le voleur!*"

Alfie shrank back in fear. The sight of the knife jutting from the photographer's shirt pocket reminded him of their last encounter. But Penelope wasn't here to help him now.

"Why do you still plague me?" Jacques Le Prince asked, advancing on Alfie with a snarl. "Hasn't Eddie Gold stolen enough from me already? This is all I have left."

"You don't understand," Alfie stuttered, desperately searching for the words that would quell the Frenchman's fury. "I'm no thief. I've just come here to find out the truth about Edward Gold's invention. What can you tell me about the Véritéscope?"

This question stopped Jacques Le Prince in his tracks. A momentary look of confusion crossed the photographer's face, then his shoulders sagged as if the burden that he had been carrying had finally become too much for him.

"The Véritéscope is mine," he replied, the gleam of anger in his eyes now dulled to a weary spark. "Eddie Gold stole it from me."

XXI

"We used to be partners, you see," Jacques explained, lifting his hand to gesture around the shabby interior of the sideshow booth. "Eddie took me under his wing when I first came looking for work on the fair."

He rested his hand again on the boxlike device fixed to the tripod. "All I had then was this camera—my father's invention—but when Eddie saw the pictures I could take, he said we would make our fortune together."

"Your father?" Alfie asked.

"*Oui*," Jacques replied. "My father was Louis Le Prince. In France he had studied biology, chemistry, painting, and photography: the science and the art of life. When he came to this country, he met my mother and, after my brother and I were born, he found work as a portrait photographer, but then one day he made the discovery that would change all our lives. When developing a family portrait in his darkroom, my father noticed on one plate of film a shadowy figure lurking at the back of the picture where no actual figure had stood. On looking more closely, he saw that this was his own father—my grandfather—who had died some ten years before."

The photographer paused for a moment to push his glasses back up his nose. "At first my father endeavored to capture this ghostly presence again, taking countless photographs without success. Then he made the momentous decision to harness the power of science to solve this great mystery. He sought to invent a camera that could peer beyond this mortal realm with every click of the shutter and photograph the spirits of the dead. My father toiled for years, investigating the alchemy of light and sound, experimenting with different lenses and chemical processes before he invented this prototype camera which could capture these ghosts on film."

Alfie listened intently, trying to follow Jacques's explanation, but in truth struggling to believe a fraction of what he said. Since the camera had been invented, countless charlatans had claimed that they could photograph the dead, but each and every one had been exposed as a fraud. Was Jacques just another of these fly-by-night con artists trying to swindle grieving widows out of their life savings?

"But my father's invention was greeted with

derision," Jacques continued, his words echoing Alfie's own doubts. "His friends and colleagues refused to believe that the spirit photographs he produced were more than mere trickery. Brokenhearted, my father returned to his workshop, vowing that this time he would create a camera that would make the world believe the wonders that he'd seen. After countless more months of experimentation, he made yet another breakthrough: a camera that could take a flurry of photographs every second—the first moving pictures the world had ever seen, long before Lumière and Edison invented their cinematographic devices. Unlike my father's first prototype, this moving picture machine did not appear to glimpse the afterlife, but the sights that it showed made everyone who saw it weep with astonishment. The magic of reality captured forever on a reel of film. He shot countless sequences—street scenes and city life—even a film of my brother and me playing in the garden."

A slight dampness appeared in the corners of the Frenchman's eyes, his voice cracking slightly as he continued to speak. "My father saw that this new invention could make him his fortune and planned to travel to America to patent his machine and demonstrate its wonders to the public at last. He sent my mother and brother ahead, whilst I stayed behind with the intention of following them all as soon as I had completed my studies. However before my father departed for America, he traveled to France to visit my uncle there and, somewhere on his return, the terrible fate befell him that tore my family apart."

The photographer's voice had dropped to a whisper, the words almost too painful to utter. "My father never stepped off the train in Paris— he simply disappeared. The police called it suicide, but I know that he would never have deserted us, not on the eve of his dream coming true. They never found his body, and all his possessions, including his cinematographic invention, were lost too." Jacques glanced up to meet Alfie's gaze, a reluctant tear running down his cheek. "That was ten years ago now. My mother and brother were stranded on the other side of the ocean, whilst all I had left of my father was this first prototype camera. No money, no family, no home. I was lost."

Alfie shifted uncomfortably as Jacques unburdened himself of a decade of grief. His tale sounded more like a plot from the pages of the *Penny Dreadful* with its stories of ghosts and strange disappearances. A worry itched at the back of his brain. What exactly was Penelope caught up in here?

As if sensing his unease, Jacques now began to explain how the partnership of Gold & Prince Pictures had come to be.

"As many who fall on hard times do, I drifted to the fair, hoping to lose myself in its maelstrom.

179

I had the vaguest notion of offering my services as a fairground photographer, and when Eddie took an interest in my talents, I thought I had found a true friend. When he saw the pictures I could take with my father's still camera, Eddie threw his flea circus out into the fields and transformed his sideshow booth into Gold & Prince Pictures—spirit photographers extraordinaire."

Jacques ran his fingers through his close-cropped hair. "I promised myself that as soon as I had saved enough money I would travel to America to be with my family again, but somehow with Eddie in charge, there was never enough." He let out a bitter laugh. "I trusted him then—fool that I was."

Alfie tapped his foot impatiently, small clouds of sawdust rising from the floor. He couldn't wait any longer. "But what about the Vérité́scope?"

In response to this question, a bitter smile played across Jacques's lips. "Eddie started to worry that my portraits of the afterlife were losing their appeal," he replied. "As he stood outside the booth he saw the crowds queuing for the newfangled cinematograph shows: the Bioscope booths and Phantasmagoria. I tried to reassure him, told him that these moving picture shows were pale imitations of my father's last and greatest invention, but this only seemed to enrage him. Eddie called me a liar and challenged me to prove what I said. He said that if my father's machine had been as great as I claimed, then it would make me enough money to buy a thousand tickets to America. All I had to do was invent it again."

The photographer's eyes narrowed behind his half-moon glasses. "I couldn't let such an insult go unanswered. Burying myself in the darkroom at the back of this booth, I set about trying to recreate my father's last invention. By building a brand-new camera, even improving on my father's design, I would show Eddie Gold the truth of my words. First, through a wearying process of trial and error, I discovered a way to replicate the chemical composition of the film from my father's still camera. Transferring this to a cinematograph reel, I found that by modifying the mechanisms of a conventional camera I could increase the frame rate by a thousandfold, producing flawless moving pictures, whilst the addition of chromatic filters and magnetic recording apparatus enabled the capture of color and sound as well. But that wasn't all. Turning the camera's winder for the very first time, I made the most marvelous discovery."

Jacques's hands traced strange patterns in the air as if reliving this moment again. "As I looked through the viewfinder onto the scene of the bustling fair, I saw a miraculous sight. Strange shadowy figures flitted amongst the crowds; ghosts stalking the footsteps of those who still lived. With this invention, I had finally solved the riddle of death. I could see the souls of the departed separated from the living by the merest of vibrations; their ethereal forms existing beyond the spectrum of light visible to the naked eye, but captured by the lens of my machine. I glimpsed the face of Evangeline, a trapeze artist who had died in a fall a mere few months before, and as she looked into the camera lens I knew she could see me too. Emboldened, I tried to speak to her, but although her lips moved in reply, I could not hear her words, and when the reel of film ran out, her shadow disappeared as though it had never been there."

His eyes gleamed brightly behind his gold-rimmed glasses. "Every night I repeated this experiment, turning my camera towards all the corners of the fair and then watching as the ghosts of the past wandered like shadows through its frame: the freaks and the mountebanks, bare-knuckle fighters and long-forgotten clowns. I saw Evangeline again, her shadowy figure growing more distinct each time the camera fixed her in its gaze, but when I saw this, a strange sense of dread stirred in me too. When I watched these moving pictures, I began to believe that this camera's power was beyond even that imagined by my father. As well as preserving the glimpses of these spirits, I grew to suspect it could also bring them back. With the revelation of this fearful truth, I christened my invention the Vérité scope."

Jacques paused for a moment as if relieving a

painful memory. "Wishing to share my concerns, I gave Eddie a demonstration of the camera's strange power, explaining to him the fears that I had. Eddie convinced me we should set up a new business— the Alchemical Moving Picture Company—to investigate this phenomenon further. I signed the contract he prepared, thinking this vestige of respectability would help us to consult the finest scientific minds in the country, but realizing too late that Eddie had his own plans." Jacques shook his head. "When I learned what he wished to do, I tried to persuade him of its folly, but the contract that Eddie had tricked me into signing gave him possession of everything. He took the Véritéscope from under my nose, leaving me here and setting up his own office in the heart of Cecil Court. When I followed him there to demand my camera back, Eddie threatened me with the full force of the law. With his underhand trick, he had stolen my invention and I couldn't do a thing."

His story at an end, Jacques cast Alfie a quizzical glance. "How have you heard of the Véritéscope anyway?" he asked. "Are you a journalist?"

"No," Alfie replied. "I work for the *Penny Dreadful*. Edward Gold is using the camera to make a film of one of Montgomery Flinch's tales of terror."

Jacques Le Prince suddenly paled. "What is it about?"

"Oh, just one of Montgomery Flinch's usual tales

of murder, betrayal, and revenge," Alfie replied, slightly mystified. "Mr. Flinch and his niece are down in Devon now watching Gold bring the story of *The Daughter of Darkness* to life."

"*Mon Dieu!*" Jacques cried out, his eyes widening with fear. "After all my warnings, he still persists with this madcap scheme." The photographer sprang forward and seized hold of Alfie's shoulders. "We have to stop him before it is too late!"

Wigram peered over his glasses, his sharp eyes scrutinizing both Alfie and Jacques as they stood in front of his desk. The rest of the *Penny Dreadful*'s office lay in darkness, the shadowy clock on the wall now nearing midnight. From above the lawyer's desk, the amber glow of the single gas lamp was reflected in Jacques's spectacles, the photographer's eyes behind these impatient as he awaited Wigram's reply.

"I am sorry to hear of your own misfortune, Mr. Le Prince," the lawyer began, "and these revelations about Edward Gold's conduct do cause me some concern, but I have absolutely no authority to stop the production of *The Daughter of Darkness*. Montgomery Flinch has signed a contract giving the Alchemical Moving Picture Company the exclusive rights to create this film, and he is in Stoke Eversholt as we speak, supervising the adaptation of his tale."

Leaning forward, Jacques banged his fist down on the desk with a growl. "Then we must go there too," he answered, barely able to keep his emotions in check. "Do you not understand what I am telling you? You cannot allow this film to be made. It is too dangerous!"

Wigram's brow furrowed in reply, a flicker of distaste creeping across his countenance at the Frenchman's show of emotion. "I understand that perfectly, Mr. Le Prince," he said. "You have told me nothing else since you arrived here with Alfie at nearly midnight, although I'm still at a loss to know exactly why. How on earth could a film of *The Daughter of Darkness* possibly be dangerous?"

As amber shadows danced across his face, Jacques frowned in reply. "I have told you, Monsieur Wigram," he said, failing to keep the frustration from his voice, "this story is not what it seems. I have heard Eddie speak of Stoke Eversholt before—it is the place where he was born and the setting for the injustice that scarred his young life. His family worked down Lord Eversholt's copper mine; the aristocrat who owned the land on which Stoke Eversholt stands." Jacques sniffed. "If only you English had followed France's example and rid yourself of such vermin. Anyway, one night when he neared fifteen, Eddie was out poaching rabbits when he found Lord Eversholt's daughter, Amelia, lost on the moor. He guided her safely home and, as a token of her gratitude, Amelia gave him a gift of a precious stone, a family heirloom. However, when Lord Eversholt discovered this, he flew into a rage, accusing Eddie of theft and beating him to within an inch of his life; then when Amelia cried out in protest he took his whip to her as well. Banished from Stoke Eversholt, Eddie fled to London, eventually finding his way to the fair, whilst the next that he heard of Amelia was when his family sent word that she had passed away, only weeks after he had left. Consumption they said, but Eddie knew the truth."

Jacques pushed his glasses back up his nose, staring at Wigram with an unsettling intensity. "I learned all of this from Eddie himself, less than a year ago. When he saw the newspaper reports of Lord Eversholt's passing, I heard him curse the man's name, pouring out this tale of injustice, filled with a boiling rage that death had robbed him of the chance to take his revenge."

"I still don't see how this has anything to do with Montgomery Flinch," Wigram replied, shifting uncomfortably in his seat. "Admittedly, there are some similarities with his tale of *The Daughter of Darkness*—"

"Don't you realize?" Jacques interrupted. "The coincidences are uncanny—that must be why Eddie has chosen this tale. He wants to reveal to the world what a monster Lord Eversholt was, and by twisting Flinch's story he can finally take his revenge. But that's not all." Behind his glasses,

Jacques's eyes blazed with a fierce conviction. "Using the power of the Véritéscope he told me he plans to bring Amelia back from the grave. The ghosts that Flinch writes of will be real when the camera rolls."

XXII

The black jewel hung heavy on the velvet ribbon around Penelope's neck. Reaching up, her slender fingers nervously stroked the tear-shaped stone, before slipping it again beneath the ruffles of her gown, safely out of sight.

At the sound of a curse, Penelope turned to see Edward Gold hunched behind the Véritéscope, the small door on the side of the camera hanging open as he struggled to fit a fresh reel into place. As the film neared its finale, it seemed as though even the Véritéscope was reluctant to see how this story would end. The cinematograph reel slipped from Gold's fingers, its casing landing with a clatter on the floor, and the filmmaker let fly another volley of curses.

Penelope turned away with a faint sigh of relief. She could only hope that this latest delay might help her to escape the camera's gaze for another night at least. A dull ache throbbed behind her eyes as she stared into the shadows that lurked beneath the bookcases, her trembling fingers betraying her fear. Since she had seen Amelia's ghostly figure step into this room only hours before, Penelope felt as though she was being stretched thin. She glanced down at her hand, the pale skin there almost translucent beneath the lamplight. What was happening to her?

With a sharp click, Penelope heard the door of the Véritéscope shut and, glancing back, she saw Gold turn its winding handle to prepare the film reel. As she watched this, a peculiar light-headedness came over her and Penelope reached out to the bookcase to steady herself as the shadow it cast lengthened around her.

"Are you quite all right, Miss Tredwell?"

As quickly as it had come, the dizziness passed and Penelope looked up to see Gold staring at her impatiently, the winding handle of the Véritéscope now still.

"I think so," she replied with a faint tremor to her words. "Although, perhaps I could sit down for just a moment."

Reluctantly, Gold nodded. Leaving his post by the camera, he hurried to offer Penelope a helping hand, guiding her toward a nearby armchair. Once seated, she looked up at the director with an inquisitive gaze. In the bright glow of the gas lamps, Gold's features seemed more careworn than when he had first stepped into the offices of the *Penny Dreadful*. His red-tinged whiskers were now peppered with gray, but Penelope could still glimpse behind the lines the features of the young Edward Gold, the face she had seen staring out from the faded photograph, hidden in the dark recesses of Eversholt Manor.

She remembered the closing lines of the letter she had found in the same bundle as the photograph: *I only hope that it will be in my power one day to return to right this great wrong*. Was that what Gold was trying to do here? But what wrong did he wish to right? When she'd returned to the room to try to find out more, the bundle of papers was gone.

Unaware of Penelope's deliberations, Gold glanced down at his watch. "Are you quite recovered?" he asked, unable to hide his impatience.

Penelope stared up at him, her face still pale, and shook her head apologetically. "If I could just rest a little while longer," she replied, a faint quaver still lingering in her voice. "I think that the strain of the day has taken its toll at last. Perhaps we could delay the filming of this scene until the morning?"

His eyes narrowing as she spoke, Gold stared at Penelope intently, the expression on his face transformed into a tight-lipped scowl. As the gas lamps flickered, his shadow quivered with a barely contained frustration.

"Fine," he finally snapped. The filmmaker turned

to leave, but before he could take a step Penelope fired at him the question that still plagued her.

"Could I just ask, Mr. Gold, why did you choose to make a film of *The Daughter of Darkness*?"

The filmmaker turned back to face her, his haggard features wreathed in shadows.

"After all," Penelope continued, "Montgomery Flinch has penned many more celebrated stories. Why not a film of *The Dread Mare Rises* or *The Secret of the Withered Man*? What was it that drew you to this particular tale?"

Gold fixed Penelope with an unwavering stare.

"*The Daughter of Darkness* spoke to me," he replied simply. "The tragedy that lies at the heart of this tale is a truth that must be told. Somehow through his pen, your uncle has breathed new life into the faded memories of the past. I will not let them be forgotten again."

As Gold spoke, Penelope caught a glimpse of the pain that lurked behind his gaze. She recalled his words to her when they had first arrived at Eversholt Manor. *"There are other stories that lurk within these walls as well. Rest assured the changes I have made all add to the truth of this tale."*

"Besides," he continued, a wry smile curling his lip as he glanced up at the portrait of Lord Eversholt on the wall, "the name of Montgomery Flinch opens many doors. I have your uncle to thank for this priceless opportunity."

The filmmaker reached out a hand to help Penelope from her seat, and as she leaned forward to accept it, the jet-black stone around her neck slipped into the light. Catching sight of it, Gold let out a sudden gasp.

"Where did you get this?" he demanded, his hand now reaching for the ribbon around her neck.

Penelope tried to move away as Gold's fingers closed around the stone, pulling the ribbon more tightly around her throat as he bent forward to inspect it.

"Mr. Gold, you're hurting me," she gasped.

Ignoring her protest, Gold stared at the jewel in his hand, his gaze as black as the gemstone itself.

"Tell me!" he demanded. "Where has it come from?"

Inside her mind, Penelope saw Amelia's face emerging from darkness, silver strands of mist still clinging to her shadow as she held the glittering jewel in her hand. She remembered her whispered words: *"I once gave you the gift of this stone. Now you are giving me the gift of life in return. I want to thank you, Edward."*

Penelope stared up into Gold's face, his dark-browed features seething with a strange mixture of hope and despair. Somehow she knew she couldn't tell him the truth.

"I found it," she replied, finally twisting herself free from the filmmaker's clutches. "It was in my room with the rest of Amelia's costumes. I thought that you had left it for me there." Her hand reached up to the velvet ribbon, feeling the chill of the tear-shaped stone beneath her fingers. "I didn't realize that the sight of it would cause you such alarm."

Penelope's answer seemed to break the spell that Gold was under, the fire in his eyes beginning to fade as he met her gaze again.

"I'm sorry," he said stiffly. "It just took me by surprise." His gaunt features were haunted by the ghost of a smile. "Of course, you must wear this, Miss Tredwell, it is only fitting and right. Consider it my gift to you for bringing Amelia to life."

Penelope blanched, the strange echo of Amelia's words making her shiver.

"And now you should rest," Gold continued, his gaze glinting as black as the Véritéscope's lens. "For tomorrow we must return to the shadow of the mine where we will show how this story ends."

XXIII

Resting his hand against the window frame, James Denham stared out across the desolate moor. Clouds shrouded the skyline and a drizzling mist was beginning to creep down the slopes of the valley. Noon was fast approaching, but the day seemed to have already turned its mind toward dusk as the sun remained a memory. James's gaze followed the black beetle-like shape of a motorcar as it climbed the winding track that led toward the distant mine. Behind the wheel, Edward Gold was transporting the Véritéscope to its final filming location.

The young actor's shoulders gave a shudder as from the corridor the echoing sound of footsteps drew near. Monty's face peered around the doorframe. His cheeks were flushed, but as he spied James's figure standing before the bay window, a relieved smile lit up his face.

"There you are, Mr. Denham!" Monty exclaimed,

stepping into the salon with a fresh spring in his step. "So this is where you've been hiding. I have been looking everywhere for you. We must depart at once for the mine. Once this final scene is filmed, we can all leave this godforsaken place and get back to the bright lights of London at last."

Monty rested his hand on the young actor's shoulder and then recoiled in surprise as James turned to reveal the tears streaming down his face. "Good grief, what on earth is the matter?"

In reply James slowly shook his head, unable to speak of the fear that lay within his heart. That morning he had watched Gold film the final argument between Amelia and her father, Lord Eversholt—the encounter where his character's terrible fate would be sealed. As Monty and Penelope delivered their lines, he had felt an icy hand rest on his shoulders and then heard the whisper of Amelia's voice in his ear.

"Edward..."

With a yelp of alarm, James had almost jumped out of his skin, his panicked cry bringing the scene to an abrupt close. Turning from the Vériteéscope, Gold had fixed him with a murderous glare.

"Get out!" he had snapped. "Get out!" But James hadn't needed telling twice as he fled from the library and the shadows that lurked there. Now, as he met Monty's worried gaze, he fumbled for the words to explain his fear.

"I don't think I can carry on, Mr. Flinch. This

story of yours is haunting me. I must leave before it's too late."

Monty frowned. Without James, how could they film this final scene when the boy's presence was demanded on every page of the script? The prospect of how this could delay his return to London filled Monty with dread. Thinking quickly, he threw a reassuring arm around James's shoulder.

"Nonsense, my dear boy," he said. "You're just suffering from a touch of stage fright. It happens to the best of us." Monty shepherded the young actor toward the door, eager to get him on set so that he could finally escape from this place. "You'll feel differently once you're in costume. Come now, best foot forward—the show must go on."

With a curse, the driver twitched his whip across the backs of the horses' necks, urging them on through the gathering mist. The carriage lurched forward again, slowly climbing the rutted track as it neared the summit and the stone cottages that lay in the shadow of the mine. From the carriage window, Penelope stared out at the half-shrouded scene. Sat facing her, Monty leafed through the pages of his script, dressed in Lord Eversholt's black frock coat.

Swirls of mist were still rolling in from the moor, their shadowy fingers clinging to the stone tower of the pumping works—a mocking reminder of the steam that once hissed from its chimney.

But the mine itself lay in silence as, beyond the pithead, Penelope saw the ragged line of extras following the track that led to the chapel. Their heads bent against the drizzling rain, men, women, and children alike were enacting a scene they had performed for real so many times. At the head of the line, four stout-shouldered men bore a single wooden coffin, its slender dimensions hinting at the youth of the body carried inside.

Penelope shook her head, her sense of unease growing with every passing minute. The story of *The Daughter of Darkness* had reached its final page, where Oliver would rise from his grave to take his revenge on Lord Eversholt. But as Edward Gold stood waiting on the steps of the tiny chapel, his camera trained on the approaching mourners, Penelope fervently wished that she had never written the tale.

As the mist flowed and eddied around the wooden crosses surrounding the chapel, the coffin-bearers picked a path toward a freshly dug grave. Sheltering there beneath an umbrella, ready for his resurrection from the dead, James waited. His face was caked in make-up that gave his skin a deathly pallor, a pale blue rim running around his mouth and his eyes, while his gaze searched the gathering mist.

With a nervous whinny, the horses were reined to a standstill, the carriage lurching to a halt some twenty feet from the grave. Monty glanced up in surprise.

"Are we here?"

Hidden beneath the folds of her black shawl, Penelope clasped the jet-black stone tight. She slowly nodded her head, trying not to betray the fear running through her veins.

From his vantage point, Gold lifted his gaze from the viewfinder, carefully checking that everyone was in position before he turned the handle to roll the film for the final time. The bark of his voice cut through the mist, a single word that sent a shiver of electricity through everyone who heard it.

"Action!"

Pushing past Penelope, Monty reached for the door with a sigh. "Once more unto the breach," he muttered, "and then we can get out of this blasted place at last."

Monty flung open the door and, as the mists swirled around him, he climbed down from the carriage, snatching the whip from the hand of the driver as he went. Raising his arm, he gave it an experimental snap and, in reply, the horses shied skittishly away. A devilish grin spread across Monty's features. He may as well send the old villain off in style. Stepping forward, he surveyed the huddled band of mourners now gathered around the open grave.

The coffin was being lowered into the pit, the bearers' hands braced against the straps as it slowly disappeared from sight. Ignoring this and all conventions of common decency, Monty didn't break his stride, swishing the riding crop in front of him as he stepped through the swirling mist.

"Get back to work," he snarled, "else I'll take my whip to the rest of you. That copper won't mine itself!"

The sullen faces of the extras turned toward him, a glowering hatred hidden behind every pair of eyes. They remembered all too well Lord Eversholt's cruelty, forgetting for this moment that it was Monty standing there in his stead. As the rain fell like tears across the graveyard, Monty raised his arm with a growl, the whip flashing back, ready to strike.

This was Penelope's cue. Leaning forward, she reached for the carriage door, but then fell back in her seat as a sudden dizziness stole over her again. Her mind reeled, gripped by panic as this strange sensation seized her. Through fluttering lids, she saw the carriage fill with shadows, the ghostly figure of Amelia Eversholt looming before her in the gloom.

Soft curls of hair framed her deathly pale features, the girl wearing the same gray gown as when Penelope had first glimpsed her in the shadows of Eversholt Manor, somehow more real now than ever before. With a spectral hand, Amelia reached out toward Penelope, her ashen fingers stealing toward the jet-black stone.

"Thank you," she breathed as she lifted it from Penelope's grasp. "It's time for *you* to sleep now."

Penelope tried to speak, but no words came; her limbs seemed heavy and lifeless as she sat there in a daze. Powerless, she watched as Amelia turned to step down from the carriage; the ghostly figure taking her place at last. As the mists swirled around her, Amelia walked toward the open grave, gliding past Monty as if he wasn't even there.

"I have returned," she said, as the figures huddled around the grave watched her through fearful eyes. "You have all suffered at my father's hands, but now it is time to put right the wrong that was done." In her right hand she held up the obsidian stone, the jewel shimmering with an unearthly light. Amelia's eyes glittered darkly and, when she spoke again, her words came out in a hiss. "Let us take our revenge at last."

With a sweeping gesture, Amelia cast the stone into the open grave.

For a second there was silence, the only sound that could be heard the distant whir of the Véritéscope. Then a pale hand thrust its way free from the grave and James's ghostly features rose to greet them, the boy shaking the earth from his shoulders as he climbed out of the open pit.

"It can't be," Monty cried in mock surprise, little realizing that it wasn't Penelope who had summoned this counterfeit ghost. "You're dead, I tell you, dead! I heard your neck break when I pushed you down the pit."

James's gaze burned with an unearthly light

as, clutching the stone, he moved toward Monty with a relentless tread. Letting out a low whimper, Monty scrambled backward, trying to reach the sanctuary of the carriage, his long frock coat trailing in the mud.

From his vantage point on the chapel steps, Gold still turned the winding handle, his eye fixed to the camera's viewfinder. The noise of the Véritéscope seemed to be growing louder with every passing second; wisps of what looked like smoke were seeping from the corners of its casing. The camera's whir was turning into a whine—a strange humming sound that filled the air as it reshaped reality around them.

From the graveside, the huddling mourners had fallen into step behind James—an avenging Pied Piper at the head of his horde. All around him, the faces of men, women, and children alike shone with the same hatred; the strange power of the Véritéscope twisting their minds to unleash their true desires at last. Long memories of brutish lifetimes spent toiling down the copper mines, slaving to fill Lord Eversholt's pockets, came back to them. Now was their chance for revenge.

Still frozen in her seat, Penelope watched as Monty tried to scramble up the steps of the carriage. It was as though she was looking at him through the wrong end of a telescope, the world outside slowly shrinking from view as shadows filled her mind. Just before arms reached up to drag him back, Monty caught a glimpse of her face framed in the window. In confusion, he glanced back at Amelia's ghostly gray silhouette.

"Wait!" he cried out. "Who are you?"

Hoisting his struggling body between them, the muddied tails of his frock coat twisting in the wind, the four coffin bearers turned with a lumbering gait to follow James, the pale figure of the boy already picking his path back to the grave he had risen from. As the rain flattened her raven curls, Amelia turned to watch this macabre procession, a malevolent grin splitting her shadowy features.

"Unhand me!" Monty cried with real fear in his voice. "Let me go!"

The ragged crowd swarmed around him, hauling Monty toward the beckoning grave. Struggling wildly, his eyes darted across their faces, searching for the one person who could save him. As his spread-eagled form was hoisted over the empty pit, Monty let out a loud wail of terror.

"Penelope!"

Trapped inside her own mind, Penelope could only watch helplessly as the horrors of the tale came to life; the lines of the script leading inexorably toward the grisly end Gold had penned. She had to stop this somehow. Struggling to shake the strange lethargy that still clung to her limbs, Penelope tried to stand, swaying for a moment on the carriage's step before falling in a swoon.

As Monty's despairing cries rent the air, Penelope lay there slumped in the mud, her waxen features wreathed in shadows.

The villagers were crowded around the empty grave, Amelia's spectral form standing at its head. Still struggling, Monty was pitched forward into the pit, the rain-sodden earth breaking his fall. He scrambled to his feet. Glancing around him, Monty's eyes widened with fear as, in the darkness of the grave, he caught a glimpse of another shadowy form. Reaching up, he tried to pull himself free, his hands scrabbling against the side of the hole, but the ground just crumbled beneath his fingers.

"Help me!" he cried, his mud-smeared face staring up in despair.

A hideous whine filled the air as Amelia reached down to pick up a handful of earth, the dirt falling from her shadowy fingers as she scattered it into the grave with a sigh.

"Ashes to ashes, dust to dust."

Following her lead, James and the others cast their own handfuls into the pit, the earth showering down on Monty as he cried out in anguish.

"Please, I beg of you—no!"

Then from the track came the clatter of horses' hooves. As she lay in the shadow of the carriage, Penelope saw a cart lurch to a halt at the roadside. Perched next to the driver, she caught a glimpse of her guardian, Mr. Wigram, staring over his spectacles in surprise at the scene that greeted them.

Penelope tried to lift her hand, but then stared in horror at her translucent fingers, the sky almost visible through her skin. "Help me," she breathed, the whisper of her words lost on the wind.

From the back of the cart, Alfie swung himself to the ground. Scrambling through the thickening mist, he followed the sound of Monty's voice, the fear he could hear driving him forward. Behind him, a second man had sprung down from the cart. Rain misted his spectacles and Jacques Le Prince peered through them with a look of consternation. As Alfie plunged into the throng of mourners, trying to battle his way to the graveside, Jacques darted in the opposite direction, heading for the steps of the chapel where Edward Gold stood.

Gold was already starting to rise from behind the film camera as the Frenchman bounded up the stone steps, seizing hold of the filmmaker by his collar. At this affront, Gold's features convulsed with rage, regarding Jacques Le Prince with a murderous glare.

"You're too late!" he hissed, his hands reaching for the younger man's throat. "Look, Amelia walks amongst the living once more!"

In the shadow of the chapel, the two men fought, their tussling figures shrouded by swirling mists and the smoke now billowing from the Véritéscope.

All the while, the cold eye of the camera stayed fixed on Amelia; the shadows that clung to her slowly melting away as each fresh handful of earth filled the grave.

"Alfie, thank God!" Monty cried.

Down on his knees, Alfie leaned over the edge of the grave, reaching with an outstretched hand toward Monty's cowering form and the ghost of Lord Eversholt looming behind him in the darkness. Fresh soil rained down, momentarily blinding Alfie as, from across the moor, the sound of an anguished cry rang out.

In an instant, the incessant whine that had filled the air fell silent. Brushing the dirt from his eyes, Alfie looked up to see Amelia's wraithlike figure melting into mist, her mouth opened wide in a silent scream. As she faded into oblivion, the boy by her side slowly shook his head as if waking from a dream. James's make-up was beginning to run, the drizzling rain revealing the face of the actor beneath as the villagers looked on in confusion. The ghosts were gone and bewilderment filled every gaze, replacing the unearthly light that had been shining there only seconds before. As the earth fell from their fingers, dropping harmlessly by the graveside, Alfie reached down to haul Monty from the pit.

The actor's mud-splattered face stared up at him through a veil of tears. "I thought I was going to die!" he wailed.

Crawling free from the edge of the grave, Monty collapsed on the ground in a blubbering heap.

Alfie bent over him, fear still pumping through his veins. "Where's Penelope?"

Lifting his head, Monty waved his arm in the direction of the road. "The carriage," he groaned.

As Alfie turned to look back, he heard the roar of an engine firing into life and then saw a motorcar rolling down the track. He caught a glimpse of Edward Gold behind the wheel, the filmmaker throwing the car around the bend as it accelerated out of sight. Left behind in the shadow of the carriage, he saw Penelope lying on the ground, her features cast in a ghostly pallor.

Alfie set off at a run, pushing his way through the throng to Penelope's side. Wigram was already kneeling beside her, the elderly lawyer letting out a deep sigh of relief as she finally opened her eyes. Penelope pulled herself into a sitting position, color slowly returning to her cheeks as she looked up into Alfie and Wigram's worried faces. Around them the mist was starting to clear, sunlight breaking through a crack in the clouds and warming her skin.

"Are you all right?" Alfie asked.

Penelope nodded. "I think so," she replied, glancing down at her hands as if to reassure herself they were still there. "What are you doing here? Where's Gold?"

"He's gone," Alfie said, gesturing toward the

road. "There's no way we can catch him in that motorcar he was driving. He'll be halfway back to Exeter before we even reach the station."

Wigram frowned. "And where exactly is Monsieur Le Prince?" he asked. "Has he at least managed to recover his invention?"

Rising to his feet, Alfie craned his neck in search of the Frenchman. On the steps of the chapel, a single figure was slowly getting to his feet. Beneath his spectacles, a bloodied cut stained Jacques's cheek, but of the Véritéscope there was no sign; only ragged tendrils of mist were left lurking where the camera had once stood.

XXIV

Penelope stared at the stack of galley proofs spilling out from her in-tray, the pages of the September edition of the magazine spreading across her desk. She picked up the cover proof from the top of the pile, the paper crisp beneath her fingers. Below the banner of the *Penny Dreadful*, Edmund Sullivan's striking illustration showed a mist-shrouded forest alive with eyes. The artist's intricate inking captured the malevolent gazes of the inhuman creatures who stalked the tweed-suited professor wandering into their midst. At the bottom of the page the cover line declared:

Featuring the final spine-tingling installment of
"A GREEN DREAM OF DEATH"
by Montgomery Flinch

Penelope let out a sigh. She only wished that the filming of *The Daughter of Darkness* out on the wild Devon moors had come to such a neat conclusion. But last month's strange events had left too many loose ends.

As the mists cleared, they had discovered that Gold had taken the Véritéscope and the film reels containing *The Daughter of Darkness* too, slinging these into the back of his motorcar as he fled the scene. With the assistance of Jacques Le Prince, Penelope had tried to hunt the filmmaker down, returning to London to scour the fairgrounds and Flicker Alley for any sign of the rogue. But the offices of the Alchemical Moving Picture Company had lain empty, a new nameplate already fixed above the door. Edward Gold was nowhere to be found.

His invention lost again, Jacques had returned to his lodgings a broken man. And as the demands of the *Penny Dreadful* clamored for her attention, Penelope had tried to cast the troubling events from her mind, burying herself in the final pages of Montgomery Flinch's latest tale. Monty himself had spent most of his time recuperating in the bar of his gentlemen's club, trying to drown the memories of his premature burial in the bottom of a glass. All his engagements as Montgomery Flinch had been canceled—his state of mind too fragile to risk a public appearance. The newspapers had already started sniffing around for the reason why, and, as Penelope placed the *Penny Dreadful*'s cover back on top of the pile, she could only hope that he would soon make a full recovery.

She pressed her hand to her temple as a woozy sensation crept over her. Penelope stared down at the desk, the grain of the wood drifting randomly in front of her eyes. Since returning from Stoke Eversholt, these episodes still plagued her; a peculiar light-headedness lingering for moments before it passed.

"You seem troubled, Penelope," her guardian said, looking up from his ledger of accounts and fixing her with a solicitous stare. "I do hope that you haven't found a mistake in the proofs. The final galleys have already gone to the printers, and the September edition of the *Penny Dreadful* will be rolling from the presses as we speak."

Penelope shook her head, the dizziness already starting to fade. "The latest edition is a triumph," she replied. "Thanks to the sterling efforts that you and Alfie made to ensure that it came out on time." She rubbed her tired eyes, the dark circles beneath a testament to the late nights she had spent scribbling furiously to meet her own deadline, then glanced across at Alfie, whose gaze was still glued to the proofs as he read the last sentence of *A Green Dream of Death*.

Finishing the story, he pushed the page away with a shudder. "This is your scariest tale yet," he declared, turning toward Penelope with a dumbfounded grin. "I didn't think Professor Archibald was going to get out of there alive. When those creatures started to climb down from the trees…" His voice trailed away with a shiver.

Penelope blushed at this praise, but watching her, Wigram's gaze was still filled with concern.

"Why don't you take the afternoon off, Penelope?" he suggested. "With the magazine at the printer's, there are no pressing matters here that require your attention. You and Alfie could visit a museum or take the summer air at Hyde Park perhaps."

At this suggestion of a half day, Alfie's eyes lit up with delight. "A capital idea!" he cried, springing to his feet. "What do you say, Penny? We could take a boat out on the Serpentine."

With a weary hand, Penelope brushed a stray lock of hair from her face. She had too much to do. The next issue of the *Penny Dreadful* was still to be planned. There were advertisements to place, authors and illustrators to commission, but at the back of her mind she could still feel a lingering faintness.

"Perhaps an afternoon in the park would be a good idea," she replied as she rose unsteadily from her chair. "A chance to clear my mind before I start plotting Montgomery Flinch's next adventure."

Alfie grinned in reply. He followed close behind as Penelope picked up her parasol and headed for the door. Placing her hand on its handle, she turned back toward her guardian. "We will be back before tea."

Then a frenzied rapping sounded on the other side of the door, making Penelope jump.

"Who on earth?" She opened the door to be greeted by the sight of Jacques Le Prince. Behind his spectacles, the Frenchman wore a wild-eyed expression. Without a word of greeting he stepped forward into the office, thrusting a tattered handbill into Penelope's hand. "We must stop him before it is too late!"

Penelope looked down at the flyer in her hand.

The Alchemical Moving Picture Company is proud to present a cinematographic adaptation of Montgomery Flinch's macabre tale

....

THE DAUGHTER OF DARKNESS

....

World Premiere at the Theatre Royal, Drury Lane,
Friday, 3 August, at 7.00 p.m.
Marvelous entertainment!
You will not believe your eyes!
Prices: 5s, 3s, 2s, 1s

"There are posters across the West End," Jacques reported. "Every billboard and lamppost emblazoned with the news of Montgomery Flinch's first cinematograph show. The streets are abuzz with anticipation. Some even say that the Prince of Wales himself will be attending the premiere."

Penelope turned toward Wigram, her eyes wide with alarm. "But that's tonight," she spluttered. "How dare Gold do this? He has no right!"

With a pointed sigh, her guardian shook his head in reply. "The contract Montgomery Flinch signed gave Edward Gold the exclusive right to reproduce and exhibit *The Daughter of Darkness*. The cinematograph show of this story belongs to him alone. There's nothing we can do to stop this premiere."

"But you must," Jacques declared, his Gallic fury threatening to burst from his breast. "If Gold shows this film tonight then the Theatre Royal will be filled by the ghosts he has conjured!"

There was a moment of silence and then Alfie gave a nervous giggle. "I don't reckon that will make too much of a difference," he grinned. "That place is haunted anyway. Monty told me that he'd once seen the ghost of Joe Grimaldi on the stage there."

"You don't understand," Jacques snapped. "Else you wouldn't dare to joke of such things. I have spent the weeks since my return attempting to fathom the mysteries of the Véritéscope. If what I have discovered is true, then the lives of Montgomery Flinch and his niece are at stake as well."

"What do you mean?" Penelope asked. "Surely we are safe now we have escaped from that haunted place."

"Remember, the Véritéscope is no ordinary

camera," Jacques replied, peering earnestly over his spectacles to meet Penelope's gaze. "It doesn't just record the scenes that are placed in front of its lens, it captures the spirits that lurk there as well. The ghosts of Eversholt Manor now dwell within the reels of *The Daughter of Darkness*. When the film rolls, the Véritéscope will free these phantoms, but to truly live they need the spark of a living soul." His eyes glittered darkly. "The spark that lives in you, Miss Tredwell."

Wigram glared at the Frenchman, his features pinched in a scowl. "Mr. Le Prince, you have no right trying to alarm Miss Tredwell in this way. What you are saying goes against all scientific understanding. What proof do you have for these preposterous claims?"

"I have visited the offices of the Society for Psychical Research to read Myers's reports into the persistence of the human spirit after death. Not to mention conducting countless experiments with what remains of my father's equipment," Jacques replied darkly. "It is my belief that I have finally solved the mystery of his disappearance. No human hand was behind his fate. I now realize that he was pursued to his grave by the specters that his invention unleashed. All the evidence points to this conclusion, and now makes me fear for the fate of your ward. The unearthly bond between Miss Tredwell and the late Miss Eversholt was forged beneath the gaze of the Véritéscope. The camera didn't just capture Amelia's spirit; it stole a piece of Penelope's soul. For Amelia Eversholt to live, Penelope Tredwell must die."

Penelope's face paled at this revelation. She remembered Amelia's ghostly fingers reaching toward hers as she took the stone from her hand; shadows crowding her mind as an unearthly torpor took hold. As a chill shiver ran down her spine, Penelope remembered staring up through her limpid fingers and seeing only sky. In her heart the fear grew that Jacques Le Prince was speaking the truth.

"I understand the enmity you hold towards Mr. Gold," her guardian began, "but surely he would not countenance such a scheme."

"Eddie knows nothing of this," Jacques replied. "It is his belief that the power of the Véritéscope alone can raise Amelia from the grave. But her spirit is cold and, once it is freed from the cell of the film reel, she will seek out Penelope's warm embrace so that she can steal the spark she needs from her soul. Only then will she live again."

"She'll have to get past me first," Alfie interrupted, stepping protectively in front of Penelope.

The Frenchman met Alfie's fierce gaze with a respectful stare. "I admire your pluck, *mon ami*, but even if Miss Tredwell fled to the ends of the earth she could not escape from this parasite. The bond that the Véritéscope has forged cannot be broken; it will inexorably draw their two souls together come what may."

In the silence that followed, Penelope could hear the pounding of her heartbeat and felt an invisible band tighten around her chest. "Then what can I do?" she asked, searching Jacques's face for an answer.

"This film must be destroyed," he told her, his low voice laced with certainty, "before it is too late."

Penelope glanced down at the flyer, her mind a whirl of fearful imaginings.

World Premiere at the Theatre Royal, Drury Lane,
Friday, 3 August, at 7.00 p.m.

Every face in the room was turned toward hers, awaiting her reply. When Penelope looked up, her pale green eyes were set in a resolute stare. There was only one thing they could do.

"I think a trip to the theatre is in order," she said, tossing her hair back decisively. "It is time for Montgomery Flinch to take back his story."

XXV

Standing at the end of the long line of dignitaries, Monty shifted uncomfortably in his tailcoat and trousers. His hastily knotted bow tie sat crookedly amid the winged collars of his stiff white shirt, while his ordinarily florid complexion had taken on a rather paler shade.

"I cannot continue with this charade any longer," he hissed, a bead of sweat trickling down his troubled brow. "I have played the part of Montgomery Flinch in every circumstance you have asked of me, but lying to the Prince of Wales himself—that's treason!"

Standing next to him, Wigram placed a warning hand upon the actor's arm. "It would be treason to allow this show to go on," he said. "If what Jacques Le Prince claims is true, then even the prince himself could fall prey to these supernatural specters. Just remember what Penelope said. We have to persuade

Edward Gold to abandon the premiere before it is too late."

Monty's eyes darted nervously along the line. The filmmaker was already escorting the Prince of Wales across the red carpet, introducing each of the waiting guests to him in turn. Beneath the bright lights of the foyer of the Theatre Royal, a panoply of stars was gathered, all of them eager to bask in the glow of the heir apparent. Actors and actresses, playwrights and poets, the great and the good of the West End stage bowed and curtsied as the prince passed along the line.

Next to the portly frame of the crown prince, Edward Gold's pale figure appeared gaunter than ever. As the two men neared the end of the line, the filmmaker's fingers twitched, already eager to turn the winding handle and crank the Véritéscope into life. His dark eyes swept over Wigram and Monty as the Prince of Wales came to a halt in front of them both.

"Your Royal Highness, may I introduce…" His voice trailed away as his gaze reached Monty's face. A flash of surprise crossed Gold's features and for a moment he stood there frozen, staring at Montgomery Flinch with a barely concealed fury.

"Ahem," the Prince of Wales coughed to clear his throat. "You were saying, Mr. Gold?"

Recovering himself, the filmmaker forced his frown into a tight-lipped smile.

"Your Royal Highness, may I introduce you

to Mr. Montgomery Flinch—the author of *The Daughter of Darkness*."

As Monty bowed his head, the bald, bearded figure of the Prince of Wales stared back at him with a gleam in his blue-gray eyes.

"Montgomery Flinch, eh?" the prince declared, his voice suddenly booming across the foyer. "So you're the fellow who has half of my staff at Sandringham jumping out of their skin whenever they read the *Penny Dreadful*." He leaned toward Monty with a conspiratorial air. "I must admit, Mr. Flinch, that I much prefer to read the horse-racing pages of the *Sporting Life* rather than any of these so-called literary magazines, but that new story of yours has me gripped."

Under his heavy lids, the prince's gaze shone with an inquisitive gleam. "You'll have to tell me this though, how on earth will that chap Archibald escape from the creatures by the end of the tale? Those inhuman swine have him trapped with no way out."

Behind the rictus of his smile, a distinct look of panic flickered across Monty's features.

In the haze of the days he'd spent holed up in his club, Monty hadn't yet gotten around to reading the final installment of Montgomery Flinch's latest tale. The means by which Professor Archibald orchestrated his escape in *A Green Dream of Death* was as much of a mystery to him as it was to the prince.

As Wigram looked on with an expression of concern, Monty scrabbled for the right answer to give.

"Your Royal Highness," he stuttered, "I'm sure that you wouldn't want me to spoil the hidden twist in my tale for you. After all, if you read the final installment, you will surely spot the cunning trick Professor Archibald employs to make good his escape."

Unused to being refused any request, the prince stared back at Monty with a look of surprise. His portly frame strained at the buttons of his jacket, the immaculate tailoring just about containing the royal paunch. Then, with a hearty roar of laughter, he clapped Monty on the shoulder.

"Read the final installment, you say," he chuckled. "I think, Mr. Flinch, that you will be asking me next for a royal warrant of appointment for the *Penny Dreadful*."

With a relieved grin, Monty quickly nodded his head in reply. "That would be most kind of you, Your Highness."

"Perhaps, Mr. Flinch, perhaps," the prince replied with a sparkle in his eye. "If this cinematographic showing of your story lives up to the pages that I've read, then I'll speak to the lord chamberlain on your behalf."

"And as the show is now due to begin," Gold cut in with an icy tone, "I really should escort you to the royal box, Your Highness."

"Of course, of course," the prince agreed, clapping his hands together with delight. "We must see this marvelous entertainment of yours."

From behind the closed doors of the auditorium, the restive sounds of the audience waiting inside could be heard.

"This way please, Your Highness," Gold said with a gesture toward the red-carpeted staircase that climbed from the foyer. But as the prince and his retinue stepped toward it, Wigram reached out to grasp hold of Gold's arm.

"If we could just have a brief word first, Mr. Gold," he began, "there is a rather pressing matter that Mr. Flinch wishes to discuss with you."

Shaking Wigram's hand from his sleeve, the filmmaker cast the elderly lawyer a contemptuous glance. "You will have to be brief," he replied curtly. "I have given the cinematograph operator strict instructions to commence the show at seven."

Composing his features, Gold turned back to face the prince. "If Your Highness would care to take your seat in the royal box," he said. "I will join you before the curtain goes up."

Raising his eyebrow at this unexpected breach of etiquette, the Prince of Wales took his leave with a grunt of farewell. As he bustled toward the stairs with his courtiers in tow, his gaze lingered admiringly on the pictures that lined the walls of the foyer, photographs of the famous actresses who had graced the theatre's stage.

With the prince now out of earshot, Edward Gold rounded on Monty and Wigram with a snarl. "How dare you!" he growled, his dark eyes blazing with anger. "You have no right to be here."

While Monty quailed, Wigram calmly reached into the pocket of his jacket and drew out an envelope. With a shake of his head, he placed this letter in the filmmaker's hand.

"Mr. Flinch has every right," he replied. "He wrote the story of *The Daughter of Darkness* and, as this letter explains, he has now withdrawn his permission for you to exhibit your cinematographic adaptation with immediate effect. This premiere must be canceled at once."

Glancing down at the letter, Gold laughed out loud. "The story of *The Daughter of Darkness* is *mine*. The contract that Montgomery Flinch signed was watertight—I made sure of that." Ripping the envelope in two, he thrust the torn pieces back into the lawyer's hand. "Now if you're going to stay, I'd advise you to make your way to the stalls—the film is about to begin."

Turning on his heel, Gold started for the stairs, but before he had even taken two steps, Monty had blocked his path.

"You don't understand what you're doing," he said, his voice trembling with fear. "That infernal film of yours is too dangerous to be shown. You saw for yourself the demons it unleashed when we filmed that last scene at the mine. They were going to bury me alive!"

Gold nodded in reply, a macabre smile now creeping across his lips. "It's all part of the story," he said. In the hollows of his face, Gold's eyes glittered darkly. "And this story needs to be told."

Pushing past Monty, Gold strode across the foyer. As the filmmaker reached the staircase, he bounded up the red carpet two steps at a time, heading for the grand circle, where the royal box was situated.

"It's too late," Monty moaned, turning to Wigram in despair.

But the lawyer's gaze followed Gold through the shadows as he climbed the grand staircase. Beyond the royal box, the stairs twisted toward the upper circle and beyond this was the balcony, where long rows of seats perched beneath the gilded beams of the theatre ceiling. Thousands filled the auditorium, all eager to see this latest sensation of the age. As Gold disappeared from view, Wigram slowly shook his head. "We can only hope that Penelope has more success in bringing this show to an end."

XXVI

Beneath the glow of an array of glass and gilt chandeliers, an air of anticipation filled the auditorium; the buzz of conversation could even be heard from the street outside. Reaching up to the theatre's cream-and-gold ceiling, a sweep of three tiers of seats faced the stage, their parapets festooned with gilded garlands of flowers and foliage. In these seats, the more respectable elements of the audience sat in expectation, while beneath them in the stalls, a huge mass of heads stared up at the vast white sheet that was stretched across the stage.

Flanking the grand proscenium arch, a number of private boxes peered down at this makeshift screen, the rich upholstery of their interiors providing a comfortable perch for the theatregoers seated within. Here was the cream of Victorian society: aristocrats, bankers and captains of industry, rich merchants, and respected businessmen. From the splendor of their seats, they looked down on the heap of humanity below.

A sudden fanfare erupted from the orchestra pit and the audience rose to their feet as one, all eyes turned toward the royal box as the Prince of Wales took his place. Behind him, Edward Gold's gaunt face could just be glimpsed, the filmmaker glancing impatiently at his watch as the national anthem played. It was seven o'clock. Showtime.

As the last strains of "God Save the Queen" faded away, the audience noisily retook their seats, impatient for the evening's entertainment to begin. Then, as if in response to some secret signal, the chandeliers gradually dimmed. A sudden hush fell across the auditorium as from the darkness, a silvery beam shone from one of the boxes. Like a beacon, its light played across the stage, bathing the white sheet in a sepia glow.

This ghostly light gradually softened to form swirling patterns on the screen, the shapes shifting to reveal letters and words as the title of the film came into view.

THE DAUGHTER OF DARKNESS

As these words slowly disappeared, the image of a face filled the screen, dark locks of hair framing Penelope's sad-eyed stare. Her gaze instantly pierced the hearts of everyone watching, the sorrow haunting her eyes shining more brightly than any chandelier. With its vivid colors, the pin-sharp picture seemed more real than any cinematograph show they had ever seen and, as Penelope began to speak, a shocked gasp rippled through the audience.

"My name is Amelia Eversholt," she said, the amplified sound filling the theatre with her words. "And this is my story—a tragic tale of murder, betrayal, and revenge."

The gasps in the auditorium turned to cries of delight. The assembled audience watched astounded as Penelope began to recount her tale. In the royal box, the Prince of Wales leaned forward in his seat, listening intently as she described the workers slaving in the depths of Lord Eversholt's mine where children were chained and harnessed like dogs, the crack of the whip driving them on. The prince's knuckles whitened as he gripped the arm of his chair. He had never believed that such cruelty could exist.

In the darkness, Gold's eyes gleamed with anticipation as he gazed down at the stage. As Penelope stepped across the silver screen, he caught a glimpse of a shadow at the edge of the frame—the pale wisp of a figure that seemed to shimmer in and out of sight. Soon he would see Amelia's face again.

◆

Dressed in an olive-green evening gown, Penelope led Jacques and Alfie along the long theatre corridor. The soft glow of gas lamps set high on the walls illuminated a frieze of dancing figures, the painted panels edged with a decorative white border.

Ahead on the right, two footmen dressed in red livery stood guard outside the door of the royal box. In his borrowed suit, Alfie shifted uncomfortably beneath their suspicious gaze, while beside him, Jacques kept his head low. Fanning herself ostentatiously with their theatre tickets, Penelope swept past the footmen with a flourish.

"I think our box is up ahead, gentlemen," she called out. "I do hope we haven't missed too much of the show."

The corridor followed the curve of the auditorium, and as they hurried along it, the footmen were soon out of sight.

"From the stalls it appeared that the Véritéscope had been set up in the center of the grand circle boxes," said Penelope, glancing back over her shoulder. "That should be the next door on the right."

As they neared the door to the private box, Jacques met her gaze with an anxious stare. "I only hope that we're not too late."

After the lights had gone out in the auditorium, it had taken them nearly half an hour to reach this spot. Once they had slipped from the stalls, they had climbed the flights of the grand staircase, hurrying down passageways and corridors as they searched for the place where Gold had set the projector. Through the walls of the theatre, they could hear the crackle of amplified sound: rattling carts and the hiss of steam, faint snatches of dialogue, but there was no way of telling how far the film had run.

As Penelope reached for the door handle, she felt a muzzy sensation steal over her mind. She clung to the door for support, her fingers pale as they gripped the handle. The dizziness was getting worse with every episode, her mind filling with shadows until the strange sensation passed.

"Penny, are you all right?" Alfie asked.

With shaking fingers, Penelope turned the door handle. "I'm fine," she replied, fighting to keep the tremor from her voice. "Let's bring the curtain down on this ghost show."

She pushed the door open to reveal the plush interior of the chamber within. At the front of the box, a row of four seats were set behind the parapet on which a strange brass and mahogany case was fixed—the Véritéscope. The solitary figure of the cinematograph operator was seated beside it, his silhouette illuminated by the silvery light spilling out from the camera. This bright beam shone from the brass eye of its lens, the light fanning out across the auditorium and filling the stage with life.

Penelope's eyes were drawn at once to the huge screen; the scene she could see eerily familiar. Through a swirling mist, the figure of a girl glided across the moor, her face half hidden in the darkness. Penelope's heart skipped a beat; the strange light-headedness that plagued her was growing stronger with every step the girl took. From the opposite direction, she saw James step into the frame as the lantern in his hand spilled its light across the screen. As this brightness shone, the camera's lens slowly closed in until the girl's shadowy face filled the screen. Penelope stared into her eyes and saw Amelia staring back at her.

"Miss Tredwell!"

Penelope felt a hand grab hold of her shoulder, roughly shaking her gaze from the screen. Jacques stepped in front of her, blocking her view of the stage. Peering over his spectacles, he flashed her a warning stare.

"Do not let the spirits catch your eye," he hissed, "else they will steal what is left of your soul. We must destroy the film reel now."

Trying to ignore the shadows creeping inside her mind, Penelope slowly nodded her head. Shielding her eyes from the stage, she followed Jacques as he advanced toward the Véritéscope. Behind them, Alfie stood framed in the doorway, his gaze inexorably drawn toward the cinematograph screen. He watched as Amelia peered out into the darkness, the jet-black stone that hung from her neck glittering with an unearthly light. The same light that shone in the eyes of the watching audience—a light that now burned in Alfie's gaze too.

Unaware of this, Penelope and Jacques crept in front of the seats. The camera was fixed to the parapet, its mahogany case strapped into place with a complex arrangement of cords and ties. It would take far too long to untangle them all. On the side of the Véritéscope, the winding handle turned of its own accord—unspooling the story of *The Daughter of Darkness* one frame at a time.

Penelope glanced past the camera to where the cinematograph operator sat motionless, his gaze fixed to the screen. In the reflected light, Penelope could see his strange glazed expression. He hadn't even noticed that they were there.

Jacques unhooked the clasp holding the small door on the side of the Véritéscope shut. Pulling it open, he peered inside the camera's interior, his face suddenly bathed in a silvery glow. An incandescent bulb shone brightly within, illuminating each frame of the film reel as it whirred past the lens.

On the screen the scene had shifted again. Monty's face now filled the frame. As his voice rang out, a shiver ran down Penelope's spine.

"Let me look at you, girl," he growled, his amplified voice echoing around the theatre.

Without thinking, Penelope turned toward the

stage; the sound of his words a siren call drawing her gaze to the screen. At Monty's shoulder she glimpsed the shadowy outline of another man's face. Then the image froze on the screen, the frame flickering and then fading from view as the beam of light was broken.

Turning back, Penelope saw Jacques hunched behind the camera, its winding handle now still.

"I just have to pull this free," he grunted, struggling to release the film reel from where it was nestled amid the spokes and tubes of the camera's interior.

Penelope peered over the parapet as a low murmuring spread through the theatre, the audience's voices raised in confusion. Then, from the corridor outside came the sudden thunder of footsteps.

Gold burst into the box, pushing past Alfie as he stood there in a daze. The filmmaker's gaze filled with rage as it fixed upon the figure still bent over the Véritéscope. Snatching up a bust of Shakespeare from the pedestal by the door, Gold vaulted over the seats with a snarl. As Jacques glanced up in surprise, Gold brought the Bard down on his head with a vicious crack.

Penelope watched in horror as Jacques slumped to the floor, his eyes rolling senselessly back into his head. With a frightened cry, the projectionist fled from the room and, with a swift hand, Gold reached out to the camera and pushed the switch beneath its winder. As the handle began to turn once more, a stream of light sprang forth from the lens to play across the silver screen.

Gold turned toward Penelope, his mouth twisted into an ominous smile. "So we have reached the final reel at last, Miss Tredwell."

XXVII

Gold stepped toward Penelope, his heavy-set frame silhouetted against the parapet as behind him on the vast screen, the scene shifted again. A swirling mist filled the frame, the shadows of crosses glimpsed in silhouette as a band of mourners gathered around an open grave. Four coffin bearers stood at each corner, their shoulders braced against the strain as they lowered a coffin into the grave.

Penelope shrank back in terror, stumbling as she reached the edge of the parapet. For a split-second, she felt herself sway into the empty air. As her mind reeled, the pit of the auditorium yawned beneath her, a thousand faces bathed in a spectral glow. But then, with a painful jerk, Penelope was dragged back by the scruff of her neck, Gold's viselike grip twisting her head until it was pinned to the lip of the parapet.

As her eyes stung with tears, Penelope felt the sharp hiss of Gold's voice in her ear.

"This is Amelia's story," he whispered, his words making Penelope's blood run cold. "Now watch as it begins again."

Frozen in fear, Penelope tried to close her eyes, but she couldn't stop her gaze from returning to the screen. She watched as the dark figure of a man strode into the frame. Dressed in a black frock coat, Monty swished his whip before him as he walked toward the grave.

"Get back to work," he snarled, "else I'll take my whip to the rest of you."

Larger than life, the sullen faces of the mourners turned to gaze out at the audience, an unearthly light shining behind every pair of eyes. The projection screen shimmered, the strange alchemy of light and sound holding the audience entranced.

With a snarl, Monty raised his arm high, the whip flashing across the screen. As Gold's gaze stayed fixed on the screen, Penelope felt herself slip forward toward the edge of the parapet. In a panic, she grabbed hold of the gilded beam, but she felt her fingers sink into the stuccowork. As she stared down at her hands, Penelope could see they were starting to fade; the ghostly outline of her fingers only just clinging to life. She tried to cry out for help but no sound came as on the screen the figure of a girl stepped through the mist.

"Amelia," Gold murmured.

Unable to tear her eyes away, Penelope watched as the ghost of the girl cast a stone into the grave.

Her face was wreathed in shadows, but as the girl lifted her eyes, Penelope could see the darkness that lurked there. An expectant silence hung over the theatre, the audience waiting to bear witness to this final reckoning. As the whirring Véritéscope crackled with unseen electricity, Amelia stepped forward again, slipping through the shadows and out of the frame.

The audience gasped in amazement. The ghostly figure of the girl floated in front of the screen, her long gray gown shimmering in the silvery light. At the front of the stalls, the audience could see that Amelia was hovering above the stage; no sign of wires or rigging to create this illusion. The girl peered into the darkness of the auditorium, her gaze sweeping from the orchestra pit to the heights of the balcony as she searched for the spark of life she desired. Her eyes alighted on Penelope as she lay slumped across the parapet like a sacrificial lamb.

With a shiver of delight, Amelia began to rise. A murmur of astonishment rippled through the audience. From every corner of the theatre, a sea of faces turned to stare mesmerized, watching as her ghostly form climbed through the air.

From the royal box, the Prince of Wales looked on in amazement. "I cannot believe my eyes," he murmured. "What kind of trickery is this?"

Her mind spinning, Penelope watched as Amelia's spirit drew closer. She could feel herself slowly ebbing away and knew that if the girl reached her, then the ghost would take what was left of her soul. Penelope struggled to break free, but Gold was too strong.

"The marvel of this machine," he whispered, "to resurrect the dead and give life to this poor girl once more."

Amelia hung suspended in the air. Her dark eyes glittered with a startling light, color starting to creep across her deathly pale features once more. Meeting her gaze, Gold raised his arms high in exultation as the whisper of her words filled the auditorium.

"Thank you, Edward," she sighed. Then, with a spectral hand, she reached out for Penelope's soul.

Penelope felt an icy chill rising up through her body as Amelia's fingers crept toward her. A swirling blank vortex filled her mind, obliterating every sensation until the only thing that remained was the cold. And as soon as Amelia's fingers reached her, Penelope knew that even this would be gone. Feeling Gold's grip lift from her neck, she quickly rolled to her left, desperate to escape from this ghastly fate. Her mind whirled dizzily as she dived clear of Amelia's despairing grasp.

On the screen, the film of *The Daughter of*

Darkness still played as a pale hand thrust its way out of the grave. Then the audience shrieked again in astonishment as the ghostly form of Lord Eversholt clambered free from the screen. Shadows clung to the dark shape of his frock coat, the silvery light from the Véritéscope falling across the villain's face to reveal his vengeful features. Beneath pitch-dark eyebrows the spirit's gaze raked the theatre, searching for the face of his daughter in the darkness. Then with a hiss he took flight, his spectral figure swooping over the heads of the audience as their shrieks quickly turned to terror.

"Amelia!"

The ghostly figure of the girl twisted in the air. At the sight of her father, she cried out in alarm. The theatre rang to the sound of screams as Lord Eversholt rose to the parapet, his shadow falling across Gold's face as the filmmaker stepped back in fear.

"No!"

In the midst of this confusion, Penelope flung herself forward. She reached for the Véritéscope, the giddy whine of its motor twisting the shadows in her mind. The small door on the side of the camera hung open still, the film reel inside whirring wildly as its images played across the screen. Lying prone at her feet, Jacques Le Prince's eyes flickered open, his pleading gaze telling her what she had to do.

Penelope plunged her hands into the camera's innards, feeling her fingers melting between rubber tubes and strange frills as she seized hold of the spinning reel. With a grinding squeal, the image projected on the screen juddered to a halt, flickering into a half-life as she tried to wrestle the film free. The ghosts shimmered in the air. As the heat from the burning bulb scorched her hand, Penelope gritted her teeth, straining with every ounce of strength that she had to bring the show to an end.

"How dare you!" With a hiss, icy fingers closed around her throat. "This machine is my salvation. I will not return to the shadows."

Gasping for breath, Penelope felt herself lifted from the floor. Her feet kicked against empty air as Amelia twisted her backward, the ghostly girl dragging her with an unnatural strength toward the edge of the balcony. Her mind reeling, Penelope tightened her grip on the Véritéscope; her hold on the film reel inside the only thing keeping her from being flung over the edge. Then she heard the straps holding the camera in place snap and as the Véritéscope swung round she finally wrenched the reel of film free.

As Penelope was pitched backward, she saw the camera fall and caught a glimpse of Amelia's despairing face. With a howl of fury, the ghostly figure of the girl melted into the air, her shadow disappearing as she was sent back to the grave. Her wail echoed around the theatre. The specter of Lord Eversholt disappeared too, joining his daughter in the darkness. As the camera hit the ground, the lens cracked and its light went out for good.

Slumping against the box seats, Penelope looked up into the filmmaker's face. Gold's gaunt features were stretched in a grimace of pain as he stared into the space where Amelia had been. Then, with an agonized cry, he turned to flee. As Gold raced toward the door, a boot sneaked out from the shadows to trip him, sending the filmmaker sprawling.

"I'm terribly sorry," Alfie said as he smartly sat down on Gold's back, pinning him to the floor, "but I think that Mr. Wigram has a new contract for you to sign, Mr. Gold— one giving up all your rights to *The Daughter of Darkness*."

Defeated, Gold sobbed as he buried his head in his hands. Next to Penelope, Jacques had pulled himself to his feet, wincing slightly as he reached out a hand to help her up too. But from the darkness of the auditorium there came a rising tide of sound—a frightened clamor of voices slowly reaching a fever pitch.

Peering over the edge of the parapet, Penelope looked down at the audience massed beneath her. A panic-stricken throng of men, women, and children were beginning to push their way to the exits. The vast screen that stretched across the stage was dark, but the terror it had spawned refused to be silenced.

Penelope's thoughts raced in fear. There were too many of them, all turning to escape at once. The house lights were still down. If the crowd in the stalls stampeded toward the aisles as those in the galleries fled for the stairs, the crush could be worse than the Victoria Hall disaster. Where was the theatre manager to calm this panicking mob? Then, from out of the darkness, a single spotlight illuminated the stage.

For a moment, the noise of the crowd quieted as every face turned toward the light. Dressed in a dark tailcoat and trousers, a lone figure stepped across the stage, his face hidden in shadows until he finally reached the bright glow of the spotlight.

Beneath his bristling eyebrows, Monty blinked nervously, staring out at the sea of frightened faces. As their murmuring began to grow louder again, he raised his hand to gesture for calm.

"Your Royal Highness," Monty began, his voice trembling slightly as he spoke. "My lords, ladies and gentlemen, I must apologize for any alarm that my tale has caused you.

"Tonight, the shadows you have seen flicker across this silver screen were but ghosts of what might have been. A dark dream of the macabre: a sinister tale to chill the bones on a warm summer's night. Do not shiver in fear, my friends, or let the phantoms you have seen trouble your thoughts as you sleep."

Monty stepped forward to the edge of the stage. He peered out into the darkness to make sure that his words had been heard. Then with a gleam in the corner of his eye, Monty raised his hand high in the air. "Just remember that to banish the ghosts all you have to do is turn on the light."

With a click of his fingers, the chandeliers hanging over the stage flooded the theatre with light. Hidden in the wings, Wigram feverishly flicked the electric light switches in response to Monty's signal. Bathed in this brilliant glow, a deep sigh of relief swept through the theatre as the shadows were finally banished. Then the entire audience rose to its feet as one to acclaim Montgomery Flinch.

Penelope's hands stung as she led the applause, the thunderous ovation threatening to lift the roof of the theatre. She looked down on Monty, the actor bowing deeply as he acknowledged the audience's applause. As he straightened, he glanced up at the box and met Penelope's gaze with a triumphant grin.

Penelope laughed. After everything that had happened, it appeared as though they had both gotten what they wanted in the end: Monty standing in the spotlight as the audience's stamps and cheers rang out into the night.

XXVIII

Monty sat perched on the edge of Alfie's desk, his face set in an expression of eager anticipation as the printer's assistant leafed through the pages of the *Illustrated London News*.

"Home news, obituaries, letters to the editor," Alfie muttered, his eyes flicking across every column of print. "Ah, here we are, Arts and Entertainment." Alfie fell silent as his gaze ran down the page.

"Well?" Monty demanded, unable to endure the wait. "There must be some mention of the cinematograph show. It was a royal command performance after all!"

Glancing up from the pile of papers on her desk, Penelope raised an amused eyebrow. Since the one and only showing of *The Daughter of Darkness*, Monty had been desperate to read the notices, anxious to find out what the critics had made of his performance. Meeting Penelope's gaze with a grin, Alfie began to read the review aloud.

"At the Theatre Royal on Friday evening, the world caught its first glimpse of an exciting new development in cinematographic entertainment: the presentation of moving pictures perfectly synchronized with the speaking voice. Before an audience including His Royal Highness, the Prince of Wales, the hitherto little-known Alchemical Moving Picture Company demonstrated their production of *The Daughter of Darkness*, a macabre tale of murder and revenge by the celebrated author, Mr. Montgomery Flinch. As well as penning the tale, Mr. Flinch also took on a starring role in the production, but to this reviewer's eyes his theatrical talents appeared to be somewhat limited, as his performance often lapsed into caricature. Some of the scenes were played with passion, and the picturesque locations presented with panache, but the most striking element of the evening's entertainment came at the climax of the performance. Before the eyes of an astonished audience, the characters' flickering figures appeared to step from the cinematograph screen, to float unencumbered in the air. Though this illusion was received with gasps of awe, such theatrical tricks seem more reminiscent of the magic lantern shows of old and I cannot believe they will create more than a passing fancy for today's theatregoer. It is the opinion of this reviewer that Montgomery Flinch's fictions are still best enjoyed on the page."

Alfie glanced up from the newspaper with an apologetic grimace. "That's all it says."

Still seated on the edge of his desk, Monty had turned a rather interesting shade of red. "My theatrical talents appear to be somewhat limited?" he spluttered. "My performance lapses into caricature? How dare he!" Monty snatched the paper out of Alfie's hands. "I've got a good mind to pay a visit to the offices of the *Illustrated London News* to set this fellow straight."

From his desk at the back of the office, Wigram glanced up from his ledger with a warning look. "Mr. Maples, I would suggest that you don't rise to the provocations of the press. Such behavior would not befit Montgomery Flinch."

Monty glowered in reply, while his grumbling continued under his breath.

Penelope sighed. It was time to tend to Monty's pride again. "I wouldn't worry yourself, Monty," she began. "After all, you have already proved the man a fool."

Monty knitted his brow in a puzzled frown. "What do you mean?"

"If your theatrical talents are really so limited," she replied, "then how do you manage to make the world believe that you are actually Montgomery Flinch?"

At this, Monty's eyes immediately brightened, a broad grin spreading across his face. "By Jove, you're right," he declared. He cast the newspaper aside as he sprang to his feet. "I think that a drink is in order to celebrate!"

"And I think you will need a clear head tomorrow," she reminded Monty sharply, "when you take your turn in the witness stand."

Monty sank back down, deflating slightly as he contemplated the next day. Edward Gold was appearing before the magistrate, on trial for numerous counts of fraud, forgery, and miscellaneous deception. Counterfeit contracts, obtaining goods without payment, the unpaid hire of a motorcar—the list went on—but the star witness for the defense was Montgomery Flinch.

Penelope had gone against her guardian's sternest advice in convincing Monty to take the stand, but in some strange way she felt that they owed Edward Gold this favor. It had been her story that had inspired his twisted scheme and she couldn't shake the memory of Gold's tear-filled gaze as he stared into the space where Amelia had been. Besides, with the rights to *The Daughter of Darkness* back with the *Penny Dreadful* once more and the Véritéscope destroyed, she knew that he couldn't do anymore harm. They could afford to be magnanimous.

Penelope's thoughts were interrupted by the sound of her guardian's voice.

"I meant to tell you, Penelope," Wigram began, rustling through his in-tray to pick out a sepia postcard. "We received this telegram from

Monsieur Le Prince this morning, sent from Southampton before his ship set sail for the United States. He wanted to thank us again for our generosity in paying for his fare and let us know that he has managed to track down his mother and brother at last."

At this news, Penelope smiled. At least there was the prospect of one happy ending as a result of this strange adventure. Jacques had promised her that he would leave all thoughts of the Véritéscope behind. Start a new life with his family, away from the darkroom and the cinematograph.

"Where are they?" she asked.

"They are living in California," Wigram replied. "A small village ten miles west of Los Angeles." He peered down at the telegram again, squinting as he tried to decipher the name. "Somewhere called Hollywood."

Have you read?

TWELVE MINUTES to MIDNIGHT

CHRISTOPHER EDGE

"This is what you'd get if you combined a good old-fashioned Penny Dreadful with the twisted imaginings of H. P. Lovecraft. *Twelve Minutes to Midnight* is both creepy and fabulous all at the same time. Put it down at your own cost." —Betsy Bird, blogger for *School Library Journal Fuse #8* and NYPL librarian

"Original, chilling, atmospheric mystery with a heroine of remarkable mettle" —*Kirkus Reviews*

"An excellent mystery in a league with Jonathan Stroud's Bartimaeus, Philip Pullman's Sally Lockhart, and Eleanor Updale's Montmorency series." —*Booklist* starred review

Look for the next Penelope Tredwell Mystery...

the BLACK CROW CONSPIRACY

Coming soon